The Pepper Tree

By

Dave Freedland

Aakenbaaken & Kent

The Pepper Tree

ISBN: 978-1-938436-70-3

Chapter 1

Like the mast of a majestic clipper ship rising vertically through the horizon, the trunk and its heavily leaved branches interrupted the monotonous plane of the two-lane roadway. Interstate 405 ran parallel to Barranca Road, giving motorists driving northbound from Sand Canyon to Jeffrey Road an expansive view of the tree and its surroundings. Bordered by asparagus fields, Barranca was seldom traveled, but the pepper tree announced its presence, and the density of its foliage shielded the most unspeakable of crimes.

By day the tree was odd; almost enigmatic. Why one, rather than a row? By night, it was an ominous adversary; in particular, to the officers of the graveyard shift. Most activities observed were cars with fogged windows, or simply the impromptu beer bust. But for the serial killer, it seemed to be a magnet that hypnotically drew the perpetrator toward the culminating acts of his horrific crime. It was the kind of place training officers, would admonish trainees to pay particular attention to possible ambush, proper illumination, and the avoidance of passing in front of spotlights, and backlighting you as a target.

This evening was going to prove to be the very thing about which Officer Jim Janowitz had been warned. When his flashlight revealed the woman's leg, the history of this site flashed before him within a millisecond. Serial killer Randy Kraft, had been convicted for the murder of a man whose body had been dumped at this very spot. The newspapers had sensationalized the crime by sharing that a four foot twig had been stuffed into the victim's body cavity. Two months prior to the discovery of Kraft's crime, Gerald Shill had chosen this tree to dispose of a prostitute he had shot to death. Now this.

Janowitz hit the high beams, and directed his driver side spotlight across the hood of his cruiser, while with shaking hands he radioed for back-up.

The spotlight illuminated her entire body from feet toward the crown of her head, as she lay prone, and nude from the waist down. Her dark hair, draped over the shoulders of a blue long sleeved blouse, was matted with blood that sparkled from the beams of light projecting from the idling patrol car. With his flashlight in his left hand, he got out of the patrol car leaving the door ajar.

As he awaited the arrival of what would soon become a busy crime scene, Janowitz surveyed the open field leading from the tree to the freeway, straining to see any signs of human shadows that might have fled upon discovering the approaching sedan bearing an overhead light bar. He rounded the trunk and ducked below the flashing amber caution light, carefully stepping toward the body, scanning for threats, while trying to avoid trampling evidence. He swept the immediate perimeter ensuring there was no further danger, and checked the victim to confirm that she was, in fact, deceased.

The familiar roar of an accelerating V-8, signaled to him that help was on the way in the form of the Area 4 car, manned by Officer Karl Peterson.

As Peterson's cruiser approached from the north, he could see the tree awash in the lights beaming from his partner's patrol car. The scene appeared surreal – a pale, mannequin-like figure lying face down in the dirt, at the base of a huge tree, with a slender uniformed officer standing over the body.

"You call a supervisor?"

"I phoned Austin. I heard him radio that he was Code 7 (meal) at Denny's, and figured he didn't hear my call; the reception's so bad there," Janowitz responded, gesturing with his cell phone.

"Let's get a unit to block Barranca at Sand Canyon, and another to block it off at Jeffrey. I'll call it in, and you can start setting up a cone pattern for the crime scene."

"Roger, that."

"Austin can make the call for the homicide team."

~

Sergeant Richard Austin's supervisor's unit lumbered down the pot holed, graveled asphalt of Barranca Road. The 20-year veteran was in a sour mood. Although he was the senior supervisor in Patrol, he was forced by policy to rotate onto graveyards for a three month stint, and he had just sat down for dinner when this dead body call came out. He had a feeling that he would be standing a long time, and his back would be smarting from the weight of his Sam Browne gun belt. It was day three of his 4-day work week, and it looked as if his uniform wouldn't make it to day four before needing dry cleaning. Austin slowly strode from his unit toward Janowitz after glancing at the body.

"Are you sure she's dead?"

"I checked carotid, no pulse. I looked for lividity, and saw signs of blood pooling on the exposed extremities – knees, thighs…"

"This is Irvine, Janowitz, America's safest city; we generally frown on this type of activity." Austin responded sarcastically.

The sergeant then began to approach the body, tracking across the dirt shoulder of the road.

"Sarge, careful, there're some footprints around her that aren't mine."

"I've handled more dead bodies than you've taken petty theft reports Junior."

Janowitz hoped Austin's bluster was compensation for the sobering scene that lay before them. Viewing bodies was, unfortunately, part of the job, but what appeared to be a beautiful

7

girl being discarded at the foot of this tree seemed, well, monstrous.

Austin reached over and separated several strands of the victim's dark brown hair glued together with dried blood, revealing what appeared to be an entry wound.

"Well Janowitz, looks like this young lady has a bullet hole in her skull. I'll call Homicide."

Chapter 2

Startled by the ring and vibration from his cell phone, Lieutenant Scott Hunter reached toward his nightstand grasping where it was normally placed, but the device had already fallen to the carpet. Sliding his hand to the left, he snagged the band of his wristwatch, and squinted at the dial, which displayed 2:21 am. His peripheral vision picked up the illumination from the vibrating phone, and he answered it by the fourth ring. He hated these calls, either sergeants in the field asking for a decision on a problem that they had been trying to solve for the last hour, or a homicide with minimal suspect information.

It was the latter, a "body dump." The location was all too familiar. Hunter had experienced numerous terrifying calls at that tree over the years.

After directing Dispatch to activate the investigative call-out roster, he slowly dragged his legs to the bathroom. His call-out clothes, hung separately for quick identification, included navy polo with embroidered badge and nametag, khaki cargo pants, and blue windbreaker with white "POLICE" block letters on the back. His leather gear, organized around the Sig Sauer P220 .45 caliber pistol, was a formidable weapon system deployed by several members of the Special Forces community. He holstered the pistol, added two magazine pouches, and strapped a two-inch barrel .38 Smith & Wesson back-up revolver around his ankle, and walked out the door.

Hunter fired up his Ford Crown Victoria staff car and adjusted the volume on the crackling police radio. Dispatchers efficiently rattled off transmissions ranging from record checks, to Fire Authority call-outs for utility trucks equipped with banks of spotlights to illuminate the crime scene.

He sipped a Diet Coke hoping sufficient amounts of caffeine would jump-start his efforts to clear the cobwebs. Aside from the public works personnel servicing a street improvement project, Jamboree Road was devoid of any traffic, as he headed northbound toward the freeway.

Hunter's heritage was true blue, his father having retired from the Los Angeles Police Department's 77th Division. After graduating first in his LAPD academy class, Hunter worked long enough to realize that he wanted to work both detectives and SWAT, and found that the Irvine Police Department could afford officers the opportunity to work both assignments at the same time.

Hunter exited the freeway on Jeffrey Road and turned onto Barranca, then headed toward the lights illuminating the site where her body lay. Both Peterson and Janowitz had methodically cordoned off the scene, and set up a third officer to establish a log to record the name and time of personnel entering it.

Austin approached Hunter as he exited his staff car.

"Another pepper tree body-dump for you to solve Scott."

"Well, Blackburn's on the way and he's the real wizard at figuring these out. What do you have?"

"Looks like a female, 25 to 30, bullet to the head, probably sexually assaulted."

"Any I.D.?"

"None apparent, no purse, maybe when the coroner turns her over we'll find something, but I doubt it."

~

Detective Tom Blackburn's pale blue Ford detective unit exited the northbound 405 freeway at Sand Canyon and turned left onto Barranca. During the entire 15-mile drive from his home in Mission Viejo, his mind was fixated upon this landmark. This tree had proven to be a continuing need for Blackburn's investigative skills.

Over the years, he had plotted crimes out on a pin map and determined that within a 3-mile radius of this object, various criminals with no connection to one and other had chosen this place to commit heinous acts of violence upon their fellow men and women. Can a location be evil, he thought, or was it simply a convenient spot to dispose of someone and quickly depart?

It was time to get focused and give full attention to the young woman who needed him to bring her killer to justice.

~

Blackburn checked in; then briskly walked toward Hunter who stood next to Austin's patrol car, leaning against the front fender. Despite being awakened from a dead sleep, Blackburn was dressed for business, wearing his usual short sleeve white tee shirt, tie, gray slacks, and blue blazer. With his slender 6'3" build, he looked more like a college chemistry professor. After receiving Hunter's briefing, they both silently studied the scene, taking notes, and sketching diagrams while awaiting the arrival of the coroner.

Crime Scene Investigator Andrew Norbet's camera flashed with still shots, around the body first, and then methodically fanned out, giving greater perspective of the overall scene. He momentarily wondered which photo actually captured the moment that her killer picked his spot in which to leave her. Norbet stopped, and realizing that he was losing concentration thinking about her; he continued shooting. He was conscientious, and at times meticulous, but these crimes were difficult for him to refrain from personalizing. He'd seen too many, and he was too involved in his teenage daughters' lives to disassociate them from what he photographed.

Chapter 3

Although she bore no identification, it didn't take long for Blackburn to have her identified. An arrest for prostitution two years prior produced the fingerprints needed to match the body at the pepper tree. Blackburn signaled a thumbs-up as he hurried into Hunter's office, and Hunter quickly holstered his cell phone.

"Prints came back with a 647(b) [prostitution arrest] two years ago in Newport. But she wasn't a streetwalker. This gal's mugshot looked like she came right out of central casting for a high priced call girl." Blackburn pushed her rap sheet and photo across Hunter's desk."

"What's her name?"

"Kimberly Donahue. She rents an apartment on Balboa Peninsula."

"Post-mortem shows gunshot wound as cause of death?"

"Yup, evidence of rape, but no seminal fluid."

"Condom? Possibly, but she had vaginal tears. Bruising on her chest looks like a punch, and finger marks on her neck indicate choking, but no petechial hemorrhaging of the eyes. He roughed her up, but no other signs of sexual injury."

"What was the caliber of the firearm?

"Pretty much what we had speculated. It was a .25 [caliber] auto."

"Did C.S.I. find a shell casing at the scene?"

"No, looks like she was shot elsewhere and dumped by the tree."

"Any idea where she was working that night?"

"Not yet, at the time of her arrest, she worked out of an escort service showing a Newport Beach address on Campus Drive near the airport, but they said she went freelance and hung out her own shingle."

"They give you any names of friends or associates?"

"Well, not what I would call forthcoming, but the gal I spoke with said she used to have a roommate named Sarah. You want to go with me? I'm heading down to Balboa now to check."

"Yeah, the chief will be calling me any minute wanting some updates. The Council's on his ass. I'll brief him when we get back. Meet you in the back lot in ten."

Hunter paused, thinking that the questions awaiting him from the chief would parallel those of the probing media. Several victims had their resting place before burial at the foot of this tree. Was this a new killer, or someone that another jurisdiction had been working for some time, that his team had just discovered? Body dumps were so hard to solve. Sometimes the victims were never identified. Having this one's name gave him hope that he would have her killer in cuffs soon, and save another victim from Kimberly's fate.

Chapter 4

Traffic was heavy this evening at John Wayne Airport. The lower level of Orange County California's recently remodeled terminal was designated for arrivals, and Fridays were typically jammed with cars jockeying for position to pick up family and friends. Although parking and waiting curbside was prohibited, many ignored the signs, making traffic control challenging for the Orange County Sheriff's deputies and "special deputies."

The term "special deputy" could be deceiving, and sometimes confusing to the general public. Special deputies wore tan shirts and green pants, and had powers of arrest on airport property only. Sheriff's deputies wore green shirts and green pants, and had peace officer powers throughout the state of California.

Alex Vannover was working traffic control that evening, and proudly wore his tan shirt, green slacks, and the Sheriff's Department's Special Deputy badge, which signified his ability to issue citations, make arrests, and generally keep the peace on John Wayne Airport property. He viewed the position as a stepping stone to full deputy status, but for now, was just happy to be a member of the team. The department's background investigator concluded that the twenty-four year old Vannover lacked the maturity to be hired as a regular deputy, but felt that the experience gained in a couple years at the airport could give him the requisite seasoning to attain full peace officer responsibilities.

Vannover had only left the security of his mom's Corona del Mar home within the past year, and moved into an apartment near Costa Mesa's South Coast Plaza with his high school classmate, Mike O'Dell. Vannover and O'Dell were surfing buddies, with O'Dell having the greater skill of the two. While

Alex resembled a high school fullback, Mike was the classic slender blonde with knobby knees, wearing Katin trunks and Hirachi sandals. As regulars along the southern surf spots which included Huntington, Doheny, and Trestles, they had settled in to the layback lifestyle of surfboards, vans, and hard rock music.

Vannover's mom had been difficult. As a widow whose former husband had been an accomplished attorney, she had expected more from her only son than traffic control at the airport. Instead of wearing a gun, she thought he should have applied himself better at school. Her overbearing displeasure made the transition toward greater independence a logical step. The irony of this situation was the fact that his aunt, his mother's sister, was married to a police chief.

Chapter 5

Blackburn idled the Crown Victoria staff car down Bayside Drive, as he squinted to read the address numbers. Hunter then spotted the location.

"It's ahead on the right, Tom. You can pull in behind that Porsche Speedster."

"Definitely not a neighborhood for a streetwalker budget," Blackburn stated, announcing the obvious. Hunter's stomach growled, indicating to both detectives that it was past time for lunch.

The apartment complex on Bayside Drive bore only double digits, a sign of residential opulence. Newport Beach held much of Orange County's most expensive real estate, and was home for celebrities ranging from John Wayne to crime novelist, Joseph Wambaugh. Its northern neighbor, Irvine, had gone through such growing pains as numbering homes with single and double digit numbers, in similar fashion as Newport, to demonstrate that their residential communities were equally exclusive.

The waterfront apartment structure rose above the street several stories, giving each floor a more expansive view across Pacific Coast Highway, stretching to the Upper Back Bay. A glance between buildings to the ocean side revealed a vertical phalanx of masts extending out into the Lower Bay from the sailboats neatly berthed at their docks.

Blackburn pushed the buzzer on the gang box corresponding to Donahue's apartment number, and waited for a response from the adjacent speaker. A second activation resulted in a breathy woman's voice barely audibly uttering the word, "Hello?"

"Hello, Sarah?"

"Yes."

"My name is Detective Blackburn with the Irvine Police Department. My partner and I would like to talk to you regarding your roommate, Kimberly Donahue. Can you buzz us in?"

"Is she in some kind of trouble?"

"Well, she was killed last night, and we were hoping you could possibly give us some clues as to who might have killed her."

"My God, no!! She can't be!! Where? How?"

"Sarah, please, can we discuss this privately rather than in the lobby. Would you please let us in?"

"OK, OK, wait! Can you please display your credentials to the camera overhead?"

"Sure, here's my badge, and my I.D.; my partner to my left is actually my boss, Lieutenant Hunter."

Within a few seconds, the inner lobby door buzzed, and the detectives entered, then headed toward the elevators.

Framed by the partially opened door and the doorjamb, a tall, willowy, strawberry blonde stood sobbing. Backlit by the sun's reflection off the blue water of the bay behind her, she backed away, gesturing with her hand to enter, and then pointed toward a sofa, as she slowly sank into an adjacent armchair.

Blackburn studied the girl's face, as Hunter scanned the contemporary furnishings, looking for anything that could possibly serve as a clue.

"Sarah, when was the last time you saw Kimberly?" Blackburn opened.

"She left here about 6:00 last night, saying she was meeting some guy for fish and chips in Dana Point. I never heard from her after that."

"We noticed that both you and Kimberly had been arrested for prostitution last year, but the DA dropped the charges for lack of jury appeal. Are you working girls? How do you pay for this place?" Hunter asked directly.

"That was a Halloween party thrown by some millionaire; we were partying with friends in the bedroom, when the sheriff's came in serving a warrant. I'm a legal secretary, and Kimberly was a court reporter."

"Prostitution's a risky lifestyle. It's next to impossible to profile a killer, if the victim's involved in high risk behaviors. Do you think that Kimberly met with a John?" Hunter followed.

"She couldn't have met with a John because she doesn't do that kind of thing, and we're not escorts."

"OK, so the dating service she listed for employment the time you two were arrested didn't include sex as a provided service," Blackburn shot back.

"Look, you just told me my roommate is dead, now you're implying that we're hookers. Would you please just let me mourn in peace?"

"It's not our intent to insult anyone; we would like to bring her killer to justice, Sarah. Do you think Kimberly would've written down a name, or number of the person she might have met last night?" Hunter inquired.

"I don't know. I just can't think right now."

"Would you mind if we looked in her room for anything that might help us find the guy who killed her?" Blackburn asked.

"Don't you need a warrant?"

"We're in the process of applying for one right now. In the interest of time, can we have your permission to make a quick look around your apartment?" Hunter interjected.

"All right, can I say, no, if you're venturing into something personal of mine?"

"Sure."

Chapter 6

Two hours into his graveyard shift, Officer Miles Cavenaugh drove westbound on Old Barranca Road approaching the tree. It was only one week since the Donahue homicide had taken place at this location, and it gave him the creeps. He hated this beat, with its desolate stretches of roadway connecting small villages of residential tracts and occasional strip malls. His body was not accustomed to working all night, but overtime shifts were sparse, and when they became available, you grabbed them if you wanted to save for that jet-ski.

It was quiet for a Friday night, and Cavenaugh wondered if the fog was a deterrent to the usual traffic that was noticeably absent from Jeffrey Road. He turned left, heading southbound toward Turtle Rock. Crossing over the 405 freeway would put him into Area 1, which would place him out of his beat, but he needed something to shake the drowsiness that was starting to cloud his ability to react. He would drive to Ridgeline and Turtle Rock Drive, which was one of the most panoramic views of the city lights, and he would take a walk.

Only a mile and a half from the homicide, and his attention was drawn to a flickering glow that reflected against the fogbank. As his patrol car drew closer, the glow grew to flames leaping from an object on the ground. The human body ablaze with what appeared to be some type of helmet lying near the head, flashed a blue hue at the base of the flame, indicating the presence of an accelerant.

The sight of a dead body can be startling, but suddenly seeing it in the process of incineration is horrific. In a state of confusion, Cavenaugh forgot his training officer's cardinal rule for radio protocol, which was, "think what you are going to say before you key the mike." Cavenaugh depressed the microphone while narrating his stream of consciousness:

"Unit thirty-nine, one-eleven, 10-33 (emergency) I'm at Ridgeline and Turtle Rock, and I have a burning astronaut..."

"Unit thirty-nine, one-eleven, 10-9? (Repeat), Dispatch replied.

"Unit thirty-nine, one-eleven, I'm at Ridgeline and Turtle Rock, and I have uh, uh a body dump on fire.

"Unit thirty-nine, one-eleven, copy. Unit to follow, advise."

Unity thirty-nine, Sam One, en-route from Culver and Main."

What neither Cavenaugh nor the sergeant following him up knew, was the fact that the control tower at the nearby El Toro Marine Corps Air Station monitored the Irvine radio frequency. A crash truck from their fire department was dispatched to respond. Despite the planned de-commissioning of the base, the FAA required that it remain operational long after the Marine Corps' departure.

Upon arrival, Sergeant Richard Austin (AKA Sam One) determined that a male adult homicide victim was had been dumped at the intersection, adjacent to a construction site, and set on fire by an unknown suspect. The "helmet" was a welder's face shield that appeared to have been tossed from a nearby heavy duty welder's truck, associated with the residential construction. The doors to the truck were open, a toolbox had been pried, and several tools were strewn about. Clearly, the vehicle had been ransacked.

Cavenaugh, who by now had organized himself, ran a records check through Dispatch on the welding truck, which returned to a contractor in Costa Mesa. Austin, who had since been notified of the crash truck heading their way, directed Dispatch to cancel the fire department's response, as the fire had burned itself out. He then requested a homicide team call-out.

~

It was fortunate that Hunter, who had been heading southbound on Interstate 5 from Disneyland, was monitoring the radio traffic from his Crown Victoria. Both he and Ashley had season passes, and as was their custom, had dinner in the French Quarter, caught a couple rides, and strolled the shops along Downtown Disney.

Ashley Horton, Hunter's love and co-worker, had been his companion for over a year. As a dispatcher, their romance had begun as many workplace relationships commence - flirtation, then coffee. But supervisor/subordinate situations invariably create complications, and as a result, Ashley was awaiting selection from the eligibility list of candidates for American Airlines' flight attendants. Based on the testing process, this event was imminent for the statuesque tawny brunette.

Before Hunter responded to the construction site, they decided to stop by the station first to drop Ashley off to assist with the increased service calls related to the homicide, He notified the coroner, whose estimated time was one hour before arrival on-scene.

~

At the crime scene, Hunter found Blackburn assigning five additional detectives responsibilities. Blackburn had already found that a name had been etched into the inside of the welder's face shield that was believed to belong to the victim. Blackburn's records check with the Costa Mesa Police, revealed the victim's 1968 Chevrolet El Camino had been found in a parking structure behind the Crystal Court mall. The pickup had sustained two bullet holes in the driver's side door and window, and there was a pool of blood on the concrete. There was no sign of the truck's owner.

Blackburn learned from Costa Mesa detectives that the truck's owner, Daniel Cochran, was a 27 year old welder, against whom their narcotics unit had been trying for some time to build a case for sales of ecstasy. They knew that he was selling to skinheads in the area of the Huntington Beach pier, but his source had not yet been determined. CMPD detectives told Blackburn that Cochran lived near South Coast Plaza, and was currently working the new residential construction site by Turtle Rock in the City of Irvine.

Following crime scene photographing by C.S.I. personnel, the deputy coroner and his aide lifted the body onto the gurney. Blackburn found an impression in the dirt that had been dug out in the shape of a 5-pointed star, with a large circle surrounding all of the star's points on the ground below where the body had laid. It appeared that the satanic sign of the pentagram had been used as a reservoir for gasoline to incinerate the body. However, an insufficient amount of the accelerant had been poured to sustain continuous combustion to consume the remains.

Based upon the coroner's subsequent confirmation of identity through fingerprints and blood, it was determined that Daniel Cochran had been shot to death in Costa Mesa, and dumped in the City of Irvine at Turtle Rock Drive and Ridgeline.

Costa Mesa Police detectives agreed to take the lead in investigating this homicide, while Irvine detectives would provide supplemental investigating reports in support of the Costa Mesa case. Meanwhile, Lieutenant Scott Hunter wondered what conclusions could be drawn about why homicide suspects were again pulled toward an Irvine landmark to dispose of their victims.

Chapter 7

The arrival level of John Wayne Airport was unusually busy Saturday night. The Southwest Airlines terminal was particularly chaotic with several cars unlawfully parked curbside, while their drivers sat waiting to pick up friends, family, or Uber fares. Compounding the situation were drivers stopping in the next traffic lane, blocking passage, as their riders ran to them from the curb, carrying luggage to load.

Vannover's eyes connected with the driver of a Toyota Prius, who had parked her car next to the curb, but there was no passenger in sight. As he drew closer, he could see she was a slender blonde, wearing dark, clinging yoga pants, with a fluorescent peach colored sports-bra that announced that she was serious about fitness. But her carefully appointed makeup clearly indicated that she had not yet visited the gym today, nor was it planned for the day's schedule.

"May I help you, miss?" Vannover greeted with a smile.

"I, I was waiting for my sister. She said she was leaving the luggage carousel, but I don't see her," she answered nervously.

"Well, you're not supposed to park here and wait." Vannover whispered softly.

"What do I do? I don't want to miss her?"

"Are you twin sisters? Is she as pretty as you?" Vannover inquired, smiling.

"She's two years younger, but she's a blonde with red highlights."

"Look, I'm supposed to issue you a citation, but I'll let you stay five more minutes, then you'll have to drive around again. Here's my card; have a nice day." Vannover slipped her a business card which displayed his handwritten cell phone number on the back.

"Thank you so much." She coyly smiled, while handing him a beauty salon card upon which her cell phone number had been boldly imprinted.

Vannover moved to the next car parked at the curb occupied by a middle age businessman, who was scanning the sidewalk for his wife, unaware that she was still awaiting her luggage at the baggage carousel. He withdrew his citation book, asked him for license and registration, and then began issuing a citation for the violation. The only closing statement the businessman could recall hearing from the deputy was, "press hard, there're three copies."

Chapter 8

Suzanne Duncan was the consummate city manager, having served the City of Irvine for three years with distinction. Her credentials were impeccable, a graduate of the University of Southern California's prestigious Master of Public Administration program, and one comprehensive exam away from her doctorate. With a statuesque 5'10" curvy frame, the brunette was striking in pencil skirts and open collar white blouses. She was assertive and gave press conferences rivaling those of Margaret Thatcher. Her only shortcoming in the eyes of her Left-leaning city council was occasionally failing to notify them of significant events in a timely manner.

Her downfall was set in motion decades earlier, when in 1968, the University of California at Irvine was given permission to operate a small nuclear reactor as part of the physical science curriculum. Few residents knew, or for that matter, few students were aware that this institution of higher learning around which the city had been formed, possessed a nuclear reactor. The science department designated its usage as strictly experimental, and the administration encouraged the professors to keep its existence on a "need to know" basis. However, a few years ago, the Chancellor had determined that enough time had passed to allow a local reporter to run an article recounting the reactor's use during the Kennedy assassination. The bullets recovered from the Dallas shooting had been bombarded with radiation from the reactor to determine if they had been fired from different rifles. Had the UCI professors found evidence of different firearms, the campus would be listed in textbooks as establishing one of the world's greatest conspiracies.

The tank measured ten feet across, and twenty feet in depth. Shielded by the non-descript academic building that surrounded it, the water was motionless, without wind or currents to disturb its contents. Looking down, the tank looked eerily deep, but as the control rods were withdrawn, they created ripples disturbing the image and generated heat registering on the dials arrayed along the walls.

The university has its own police department staffed by state certified peace officers; however, dispatch logs show the most common assignments involved opening doors for professors who had forgotten their keys or conducting regular security checks. These types of calls for service lend themselves to regularity which can lead to predictability. The campus cops' diligence was monitored and recorded by individuals with less than stellar intent; one such group was the Muslim Students Association. The MSA established itself as an organization condemning government interference with religious practices, while at the same time channeling funds to various terrorist groups attempting to disrupt the American way of life.

In the aftermath of the publicity, three new members at the MSA's meetings voiced a more militant perspective. Most in attendance distanced themselves, while some watched thinking that the men were testing for a reaction. The trio's abrupt departure from the meetings coincided with a reported commercial burglary of the reactor room, and the disappearance of one radioactive fuel rod.

The national news networks ran the story with experts espousing the dangers of a dirty bomb erupting at South Coast Plaza shopping center and spraying radioactive isotopes over innocent shoppers. The ever vigilant FBI's monitoring of jihadist websites found one group offering thanks to their brothers in Irvine for the advancement of the caliphate. However, apprehension of the suspects and recovery of the rods continued to be elusive.

~

The theft of the reactor rods from UCI was clearly a university specific event. The Irvine city council wanted updates, but little information was forthcoming. True, the university was within the city limits, but unless the academics called for assistance, the mutual aid contract did not kick in. The Federal Bureau of Investigation was coordinating law enforcement operations due to the terrorism implications, and their usual cloud of silence had enveloped the campus.

~

It was the end of another training day for the Irvine Police Department's Special Weapons and Tactics (SWAT) Team, and the caravan of police vehicles rumbled down Alton Parkway toward the station. Leading the column was the imposing diesel-propelled BEAR, an armored personnel carrier obtained through a Homeland Security grant. The post 9/11 funding equipped five police agencies in Orange County with assets for building the first counter-terrorist team at the local level. Among the unique capabilities of this $300,000 monster, the B.E.A.R. or Ballistic Engineered Armored Response, sported a turret for snipers, six gun ports, and a radiological monitoring device similar to a Geiger counter.

Across the street from the Alton Parkway entrance to the enclosed police parking lot were several earth-tone apartments that comprised the rental portion of the Westpark residential complex, which encircled the Irvine Civic Center. As a university town, many of the rental properties were inhabited by students attending UCI in search of that coveted University of California degree.

At the helm of the BEAR was former 18-wheel truck driver, Officer Dan Kelso, a burly red head who served as one of the team's two chemical agent operators. As he approached the driveway leading to the station's lot, a bell began ringing in the cab, alerting Kelso to the presence of radioactive material in the area. Being the second occurrence this month, Kelso could no longer assume the alarm was an anomaly.

Upon securing the vehicle into its enclosure, Kelso phoned Irvine's appointee to the FBI's Joint Terrorism Task Force, Detective Mark Kahn. Kahn ran the department's A-card system, searching for calls for service in the apartments near the station, and began matching names with persons known to frequent jihadist websites. He located a "Peeping Tom" call in the apartment complex the previous month. Two UCI coeds had reported a Middle Eastern neighbor who had been standing on the landing for their upstairs unit peering through the opening between their front window curtains. Upon arrival, uniformed officers encountered a male subject matching the suspect's description, as he was entering his Volkswagen Jetta in the parking lot.

Although he nervously denied the allegations, Mohammed al-Fayez Hazmi was listed on a field interview (F.I.) card as suspected of committing 647 (i) of the California Penal Code, peeping. Also noted on the card was his address within the complex, and a forearm tattoo of a crescent with Arabic writing.

Kahn further discovered that Hazmi was contacted by university police at 6:17 PM, two days before the reactor room burglary. A complaint called in by a female Asian student who claimed that Hazmi was following her near a science building resulted in a police response. The officer's notations on the F.I. card indicated that Hazmi was unable to produce any documentation certifying him as a student on the campus.

Following an electronic search, Kahn found several e-mail communications between Hazmi and the infamous American imam and jihadist Anwar al-Awlaki. Contemporaneous to this search, a member of the Orange County Sheriff's Department's bomb squad dressed as a meter reader walked the neighborhood carrying a device for detecting radioactivity. The spike in the readings registering in front of Hazmi's apartment prompted the bomb tech to immediately create as much distance as possible.

~

Kahn secured the judge's signature on the search warrant with few questions asked. The county's counter-terrorist Joint Hazardous Assessment Team (JHAT) assembled in the front parking lot of the Irvine Civic Center complex, dressed in Class B haz-mat suits and Patriot breathing apparatus. Joining them were five investigators from the FBI's Joint Terrorism Task Force (JTTF), along with a storage vehicle provided by the Atomic Energy Commission.

The column of police vehicles led by the BEAR, moved quickly into the Westpark neighborhood, and stopped three apartment buildings south from the target location. The JHAT operators alighted from the BEAR and quickly established a perimeter around Hazmi's building, with a 6-man entry team staging at the second story front door. The scout gave the "knock and notice" for the warrant service, and was met with a stunned Hazmi at the threshold. As the team poured into the apartment like water, immediately covering all fields of fire, Hazmi provided no resistance, nor did the other two Middle Eastern roommates challenge the commands of the team leader to assume a prone position for handcuffing.

A search of a closet in a back bedroom revealed the missing fuel rod wrapped in beach towels. The rod kept setting off alarms from the monitor held by the bomb tech assigned to the entry team. A quick call from the team leader to the commander, notifying him of the scene being secure - property located, was then relayed to the chief of police. The next notification in the chain of command would normally be to the city manager.

However she was in a closed door meeting with a finance commissioner regarding a lawsuit.

For Suzanne Duncan, the delay proved to be critical. As is typical for the FBI, the "Bureau" will often hold press conferences following significant events without notifying the "locals" who have an interest. While the Special Agent in Charge gave the details on the rod recovery to a national audience, Irvine's City Manager, Suzanne Duncan, had yet to inform the city council. She had two votes of support, but the three in the majority were looking for a reason and after a tough battle over budgets, Ms. Duncan was out of a job.

Chapter 9

Daniel Steinhoffer had experienced a short, but colorful stint as Irvine's chief of police, only to find himself abruptly unemployed when a change in the city council had left him backing the wrong political horse in the race. An election had changed the 3 to 2 liberal majority into a sweep by conservatives, leaving Democrats holding only two council seats. Law and order was the prevailing wind, and the new majority felt that Irvine's status as "America's Safest City" was in jeopardy, and that a new chief was needed in order to maintain this municipality's greatest selling point. Steinhoffer's bags were packed for Arizona, which was a temporary solution until his ultimate dream for power could be actualized.

Fortunately for Steinhoffer, the chief of the City of Long Beach, California was retiring, and the American Association of Law Enforcement Professionals was conducting a nationwide candidate search for his replacement.

Steinhoffer had been an AALEP member for over ten years. Wearing the "stars and bars" of management had been his career goal since two days following academy graduation. But of even greater significance was his having held the presidency of AALEP during a previous period of employment separation. Such ceremonial responsibilities carried weight, and enabled him to make the final interview cut, and his ability to embellish his accomplishments carried the day. He became the "Beach's" new chief.

~

"You have got to be kidding! There is no way I am moving to Long Beach."

So began another argument initiated by Chief Daniel Steinhoffer's wife, Dr. Erin O'Connell. To the members of the Long Beach Police Department the new chief may seem to lead with a management style of intimidation, but to his Irvine neighbors within earshot of his home, the doctor controlled the household like she commanded an operating room.

She certainly earned the credentials having graduated from UCLA, received her medical degree from the University of Southern California, her residency in orthopedic surgery at Johns Hopkins, and a fellowship in spine surgery at Stanford University. Her Newport Beach medical practice enabled her to charge for services commensurate with her abilities, and her luxurious Irvine home was in close proximity to Hoag Orthopedic Institute, where she conducted her surgeries.

Being married to a powerful man who was chief of police in the city in which she lived provided her with additional prestige. But moving back to Los Angeles County was definitely a step down. Dr. O'Connell had gone to school in Los Angeles and didn't like it. She wouldn't describe herself as pretty, but at the age of 50, she knew she was attractive, dressed with class, and still caught men's attention when she made an entrance.

Chief Steinhoffer, by contrast, had started to exhibit some of the pitfalls of management. Long hours, lack of sleep, poor diet, and sporadic exercise were having an effect. Taking their full measure on the chief, Steinhoffer's girth increased in proportion to his hair loss. His growing temper made it easier for O'Connell to hold fast to her position against moving, despite Steinhoffer's logic that chiefs should live in the cities that they police. So, it was settled that the City of Long Beach's chief of police would commute.

~

The insecure political atmosphere in Irvine had prompted Suzanne Duncan to become vigilant in scanning opportunities for advancement outside Orange County. When Steinhoffer left Irvine for Long Beach, Duncan viewed his appointment as a potential inroad into her securing the top position in Los Angeles County's second largest city. Duncan and Steinhoffer had met years prior at a community policing conference, and their management ideology was so compatible that she had chosen him to fill the Irvine chief's vacancy created by an early retirement.

Irvine's top management team had now been transplanted twenty-five miles north on Interstate 405, to the City of Long Beach. This circuitous promotional path would later become problematic for Irvine Police Lieutenant Scott Hunter.

Chapter 10

It was firing range day, and Irvine had the facility until noon. Under an arrangement with the Newport Beach Police Department, certain days and times of the month were designated for the Irvine Police Department to use the range in the basement of the Newport Beach Police station. Hunter and Blackburn arrived at 10:00, and met Irvine's range master. Blackburn carried the department's new Smith & Wesson M&P, 9 mm pistol which holds a 15-round magazine, and is replacing the Sig Sauer P220, .45 caliber pistol. Preferring the heavier round, Hunter still carried the Sig Sauer, despite its magazine capacity being only 8.

The course of fire was more tactical than the traditional paper silhouettes. The targets were metal, giving shooters positive, audible and visual reinforcement of the rounds' accuracy. Some were silhouette shaped, and others were disks on a "tree," designed to flip from one side to the other, upon the impact of a bullet. Shooting distances were within 5-10 yards from behind barricades.

Both officers began from 10 yards away, with holstered pistols. After several evolutions of firing from left and right hand positions, from either standing or kneeling positions, they were ready for the disk tree.

Each shooter faced a tree with 6 metal disks, 3 inches in diameter, that were held by arms that swung from right to left upon impact. Disks were stacked from high to low. The first shooter to move all of his 6 disks from the right side of the tree, over to the left side, won the drill.

Upon command, Hunter fired 6 shots in rapid succession, moving all 6 disks from right to left. However, Blackburn's first round hit the top disk, causing it to move, but it slowly returned to its original position, requiring Blackburn to fire an additional round to move it to the other side. The range master called out to Blackburn, "hit the disk on the outer edge, to move it to the other side!" He did so upon successive shots, taking a more careful aim. It became apparent that the lighter 9mm round required greater precision, and more time to move the target than did the heavier .45 caliber round.

While driving back to the station, the lesson in bullet dynamics caused Hunter and Blackburn to passionately discuss the dilemma facing officers in lethal encounters – more available rounds to hit potential targets, versus knockdown power. The truth of the matter was that neither round could consistently put an attacker down on its own, unless the bullet was placed so that it passed through the brain. That required marksmanship under duress, which was a statistically daunting task. Hunter had survived a gun battle before, and hoped he would not have to endure that experience again. He then asked Blackburn where the department was regarding the Donahue homicide.

"Well, before I get to the search warrant, we got a call from the sheriff's crime lab this morning and they said they found DNA under her fingernails. Belongs to a male, but it's not in the system," Blackburn replied.

"Interesting. The guy's probably not done joint time, or if he did, it was a long, long time ago," Hunter noted.

"The search warrant gave us her laptop, and she hasn't made a Facebook entry for the few months since she vacationed with her roommate in Cabo. She liked to post on Instagram; lots of bikini photos, glamour kinds of shots. E-mail was surprisingly business stuff, court reporting assignments. She actually is a part-time, freelance court reporter," Blackburn reported.

"Did you track down her friends off Facebook?" Hunter inquired.

"Some of them, but so far, none of 'em knew, or could confirm anything regarding her being in the escort business. Her next of kin was her mother, who lives in Ames, Iowa, and who's typical salt-of-the-earth Midwest." Blackburn replied.

"Did you find a cell phone bill?"

"Yes, and we're working with Verizon to get her most recent calls."

"I would bet her business is on that phone, and her killer's number's there."

Chapter 11

Detective Sergeant Keith Miller was finishing up his inventory of Kimberly Donahue's file folder containing bills and receipts. Known for his attention to detail, and his obsessive workout regimen, Miller's talent in major cases was his ability to organize and analyze evidence.

"I was laying out a spreadsheet on the Verizon cell phone records, when I suddenly thought that she might have had more than one cell phone. So I went back and re-checked her file folder," Miller shared with Hunter.

"I checked "S" for Sprint, but found nothing. But when I checked the file "R" before it, I pulled a "Register" bill for the Orange County Register newspaper, and I found a Sprint bill jammed between the pages that had been misfiled. She had recently opened a Sprint account, so we filed a search warrant with Sprint, and found some numbers worth checking," Miller continued.

"Any burner phones?" Hunter inquired.

"Oh yeah, as expected, but there were some that can be checked, like this one by Heritage Park."

"You want to go now?"

"The call was made the day before the homicide, but she was phoned around 6:00 PM. I think we should go there around six, thinking that the caller might be more likely to be there at that time," Miller replied.

"Sounds good."

~

As the 6:00 hour approached, Hunter and Miller were heading northbound on Culver Drive to a townhome on

Sacramento Street across from Heritage Park. Upon arrival, they met a woman in her 40's at the front door.

"Hello, I'm Sergeant Miller with the Irvine Police Department, and this is Lieutenant Hunter, is there a Michael Klein living here?"

"Yes, he's my son, is there a problem officer?"

"Well, we're investigating a crime in which the victim received a phone call from your son's cell phone."

"My God, he's only fifteen, what crime did the victim suffer?"

"She's a homicide victim ma'am; is your son home?"

"Yes, he's in his room. I'll go get him. Please have a seat."

Within a few seconds, a tall, slender teen with bleached blonde hair, wearing a Van Halen tee shirt and blue jeans entered the living room, followed by his mother. They sat down on a couch, across from the two detectives, who were both seated in fabric covered chairs, facing them, and separated by a coffee table. Miller had already activated the micro-cassette recorder secreted within the inside breast pocket of his blazer.

"May I stay here and listen? I'm a single parent and I would like to be here to support my son," Mrs. Klein inquired.

"If you wish," replied Miller.

"Michael, you're not under arrest; but we would like to ask you some questions about a phone call you made a few days ago."

Miller leaned forward, displaying his notepad, and pointed to a cell phone number he had printed on a blank page.

"Is this your cell phone number?"

"Yes."

"Has anyone else used it?"

"No."

"Where is it?"

"Right here." Klein stated, as he produced a cell phone from a front pocket in his blue jeans.

"Do you recall making a phone call to a Kimberly Donahue a few days ago?"

"I remember making a call to a girl named "Tiffany," but I don't know her last name."

"How did you obtain her number?"

"I got it from an escort service on the internet. I saw her picture on the website, they referred me to her number, and I called her, 'cause she looked like the youngest one there."

"What was the purpose of your call?"

"I was with my buddies a few days ago, and we were talking about getting a date with a call girl. We knew we were too young, but we were gonna try to "Catfish" by giving a false identity to make her think I was old enough. But she figured I was a kid, so she hung up."

"Have you ever done this before?"

"No sir, this was just an idea we came up with."

"Do you remember the name of the escort service you called?"

"It was something like Sheffield Escort; it was a British kind of place in Newport Beach."

"Do me a favor Michael. Tell your friends not to try this. The girl you called has been murdered, and you're dealing with a very dangerous business," Hunter interjected.

"We're going to need to take your phone for evidence; but I'll give you an evidence slip, and we'll see if we can get this back to you after replacing the memory card." Miller closed.

~

As Hunter and Miller left the neighborhood, they headed toward Denny's for coffee. Hunter scratched notes on his pad, and then turned to Miller while shaking his head.

"I thought that escort service said that Donahue had left, and she was working on her own."

43

"That's what they said, but I suspect that's what their standard response is to law enforcement inquiries. I'll write the search warrant to have a look at their records," Miller replied, as Dispatch interrupted.

"Unit thirty-nine Sam 3 and Unit to follow advise. Follow up Units thirty-nine, Delta 31, and Delta 32, on a possible barricade involving a domestic dispute, Number 44 Topeka. Husband assaulted wife, and ran into bedroom. Firearms are present in residence. Delta 31 attempting to negotiate a surrender. A-cards show husband 5150'd (mental commitment) last month."

Chapter 12

The assigned officers posted on each side of the bedroom door were about to experience their most acute blood pressure rise in their individual medical histories. After their failed attempts to calm the outbursts of the male component of the family disturbance, the deeply disturbed army veteran retreated to the seclusion of his apartment bedroom, and racked a round into the chamber of his 12 gauge shotgun. He then proceeded to fire the weapon into the top of the doorframe, prompting Officers Jim MacNeal and Dennis Cobb to make a hasty evacuation of the wife and 15 year old daughter out of the apartment.

"10-33! (emergency) Shots fired! 44 Topeka!" MacNeal's voice panted over the radio. Only one month prior, MacNeal and Cobb had been sent to this same Heritage Pointe apartment complex, to search for David Hamilton, a veteran suffering from post-traumatic stress. At that time, he was dressed in military fatigues with a sidearm, and was wandering in the dark, frightening the neighborhood. MacNeal's solution was to trap Hamilton's hands from behind, and take him to the ground. A subsequent 72-hour mental commitment and evaluation now seemed to them to have provided only a temporary solution to the problem.

This night Hamilton had decided to wear his 15 year old daughter's flip flops to the pool on her birthday, and instigated a family argument when she complained. After knocking his wife around for failing to take his side of the argument, she dialed 9-1-1 in an effort to bring an end to any further abuse.

~

Miller's U-turn at Walnut and Yale planted Hunter's right ear on the passenger side window, then snapped his head back violently, as the Crown Victoria accelerated toward the apartments.

"Easy Turbo! We're only a couple blocks away," barked Hunter.

"Sorry, I just have a feeling this one's not going to go well," replied Miller.

Pulling the steering wheel to the left, he brought the staff car across the lines dividing westbound from eastbound Walnut. The vehicle then slowed to a stop next to the curb, and arrived on-scene facing east against the westbound lanes. Hamilton's row of ground-level apartments had front doors opening to the street, while the second story units opened to an adjacent set of stairs.

Hunter gave a single flash of his flashlight to the officers pulling up on the opposite side of the apartment, signaling that plainclothes officers were on the perimeter. He and Miller then took up a position behind a large cable box on a grassy berm covered with large trees, which ran parallel to the sidewalk and the street.

The first patrol sergeant on scene taking command was Richard Austin, working an overtime shift on his day off. He met briefly with MacNeal, behind his patrol car, which was parked at the driveway leading to the rear carport. Austin radioed Dispatch to activate SWAT, while MacNeal returned to a position near the apartment's front door. Cobb escorted Hamilton's wife and daughter to a neighbor's unit nearby, then joined MacNeal by the open front door to watch, should Hamilton exit the master bedroom.

As more swing shift officers arrived at the apartment complex, they began locking down perimeter positions. Austin's attention was drawn to Officer Andrea Martin, an athletic brunette who had recently been assigned an alternate position on the Crisis Negotiations Team. He waved her over to the hood of his patrol car.

46

"Martin, have you gone through a hostage negotiations course yet?"

"Yeah Sarge, I finished the basic class taught by LA Sheriff's last month."

"Do you have your cell phone with you?"

"Yeah."

"Contact Dispatch, get this guy's phone number, and see if you can convince him to surrender before SWAT gets here."

"10-4."

Martin soon connected with Hamilton, and began the process of negotiations on her cell phone, while standing next to Austin's patrol car. The command post vehicle with the communications gear had left the station, and would arrive shortly. She could then transfer to a console with recording equipment.

~

Within 30 minutes, SWAT was on-scene and relieved patrol officers of the inner perimeter positions, but left Martin as the primary negotiator, since she had established some degree of rapport with Hamilton. Two of the team's snipers had been working patrol that evening, and established high ground on the carport cover behind Hamilton's apartment. However, since their sniper rifles were stored in the SWAT utility van, they deployed with the Colt AR-15 carbines carried in their patrol cars.

A lack of high-ground to the front of the apartment led to the placement of an armored BEAR on the street facing the front door, with two officers inside. One officer remained in the driver's seat, while the other staged in the turret.

Hunter and Miller stayed posted behind the cable box, preventing a westbound escape, in the event that Hamilton exited and turned to his right. Hamilton's military experience told him that the team would establish containment of his position. As he began to feel pressure and panic closing in, he spotted the sniper team to the rear.

"Andrea, I can see those snipers on the roof behind me. Tell them to leave."

The SWAT commander, now posted next to Austin's unit, turned to Martin shaking his head side to side, and silently mouthed the word, "No."

"I'll tell them that you can see them, David, but I'm not going to tell them to leave," Martin replied.

"I have an M-16 with me."

"You have an M-16?"

"Yeah."

"Well, when you come out to meet with us, don't bring it with you."

"I just want to say I'm sorry to my wife and daughter, and have you guys go away."

"You know we can't do that David. We need to have you come outside and meet with us, so we can get this thing resolved."

"You guys just want to kill me."

"No, David, we need to have you exit the apartment and speak with us. We don't want to hurt you."

"I wanted to go into Special Forces, but they said I had PTSD."

"Post-Traumatic Stress Disorder?"

"Yeah. Your SWAT guys are like civilian Special Forces."

"I guess you could call them that. They're not military, but they are sworn in. You know, some of them were in Special Forces."

"I've got an M-16 like them."

"Yeah, you said that."

"I'm going to come out with it."

"No! Don't do that David!"

"Can you do me a favor? Tell those guys behind me that I love them."

With no warning David Hamilton left the bedroom and ran out the front door of the apartment. He turned left onto the grassy berm, holding what appeared to be an M-16, military-style rifle, and moved tactically in a large circle, looping back toward the front door. In doing so, he covered eleven fields of fire established by the SWAT team's inner perimeter and sniper teams. Hamilton presented an armed threat to each of the eleven operators, who fired varying numbers of rounds from their M-4 carbines, a shorter variant of the military M-16.

Since Hamilton's route exceeded the range of Hunter and Miller's pistols, they held their fire. However, the M-4's accomplished the goal for which they were intended. Hamilton, his body riddled with bullets, fell dead on the doorstep of his home.

~

As the gun smoke slowly wafted into the evening air, Hunter suddenly realized that he would need at least five detectives to respond and form the required shooting investigation team. Policy dictated that a team of investigators from the District Attorney's Office would be responsible for conducting a criminal investigation into the officer involved shooting that led to Hamilton's death, and Irvine detectives who had not participated in the SWAT operation would provide assistance as needed.

No less than three separate investigations, including the DA's assessment of criminality on the part of the eleven shooting officers, would be initiated. Upon learning that Hamilton's "M-16" was a replica firearm, incapable of shooting real bullets, Hunter considered himself fortunate that the responsibility for the internal affairs and civil liability examinations of this event, landed elsewhere.

Still the Heritage Pointe shooting would be one more item in an in-basket already heavily weighted with the death of Kimberly Donahue.

Chapter 13

The walk across MacArthur Boulevard from John Wayne Airport to the Airporter Inn was treacherous. But evening rush hour traffic presented no challenge to Wendy Gilbert as she led a team of American Airlines flight attendants, with suitcases in tow, across on a green light that was counting down. Smartly attired in their navy blue uniforms, the four ladies stopped all traffic, except for the rental car drivers suffering from vertigo following a long flight and a broken GPS.

Wendy was a hard charging airline veteran who partied seriously after a long flight, supplemented by caffeine and cocaine. It would soon be time on this layover to substitute champagne for the coffee. The petite firecracker with sandy brown hair would be hitting the bar with her three co-workers, soon after checking in to her hotel room and a quick shower. She would be rooming with Karla Bergstrom, a statuesque brunette, who was two months out of training, and a little more circumspect in her interactions with others.

Within the hour, Wendy left the elevator into the lobby attired in her black cocktail dress and heels, followed by Karla, in teal, sporting a black patent leather jacket. Every male turned for that second look, making certain that he didn't miss anything.

The cocktail lounge was dark, and the musical trio had just begun to set up their drums, amps, and PA system. Their gig didn't start for a couple hours, but they would run through a quick sound check before grabbing dinner. The voices of approximately 10 – 15 people gave the room warmth, with mostly female conversation, plus a few male members of the cockpit crews. The tailored suits from the brokerage houses would soon make their entrances, surveying the talent, before deciding if greener pastures could be found one mile south in Newport.

Wendy and Karla selected an elevated table with four bar stools, located near the entrance, so that they would have first right of refusal for any candidates venturing into their sphere of influence. They each began with champagne to even out the lines of cocaine, ingested prior to leaving their hotel room.

Wendy signaled to Karla that it was time for a potty break. Karla needed to go too, but stayed to hold the table, while Wendy retired to the ladies' room nearby. A mutual fund broker in a three-piece suit made his move, and appropriated the stool next to Karla, shortly before Wendy's return. Following introductions, Wendy determined that Karla's new friend had arrived alone, so she scanned the room for new arrivals, who may have entered during her brief absence.

As the other two members of their team of flight attendants arrived, and pulled bar stools over from an adjacent table, Wendy's eyes locked onto the muscular athlete seated at the bar, being served his mug of draft beer. With close-cropped hair, brown leather bomber jacket, and dress blue jeans, she typecast him as military or police. She momentarily thought, "Military would be OK, but a cop might alert on the cocaine."

Sensing her stare, he turned and smiled. She reciprocated with a broad grin, and felt light-headed with a sudden rush of the drug combining with alcohol, and the butterflies in her stomach. She took a last sip from the fluted glass and rested the vessel on the table. Looking up, she could see he was standing next to her, sliding the empty stool over, studying her face as he sat and placed his mug next to her glass.

"Would you like another champagne?'

"Sure, that would be nice." She answered at hyper-speed, hoping that he wouldn't notice any powdery residue that might still be clinging to her nose. The line of cocaine she had just snorted in the bathroom stall was now reaching critical mass.

"I'm Jake."

"Hi, I'm Wendy."

He smiled, nodded, then signaled to the waitress for another champagne.

"Flight attendant, right?"

That obvious?"

"Well, this is the Airporter Inn, across the street from the airport. You're the most attractive girl in the company of several beautiful girls. That's a pretty safe guess."

"If that's a line you use, has it been very effective?" Her pupils had now achieved maximum dilation.

"I'm pretty direct. I just call them as I see them."

"Are you military?"

"I was, but I'm law enforcement now."

"Oh yeah? Where?"

"Sheriff's Department – I work patrol. Do you fly out tomorrow?"

"Yes, to Dallas, then New York."

"What airline do you work for?"

"American Airlines."

"How long have you worked for them?"

"Seven years."

"You must enjoy travel."

"Very much. Do you enjoy crime? I mean fighting crime?" She thought, "Get ahold of yourself. You're losing it." She then took a large swallow of the fresh glass of champagne that had just arrived.

"Definitely, I take pride in removing criminals from society." He then downed a large gulp of his Coors Lite, which upon mixing with his bodybuilding steroid, Dianabol, created a fresh burst of courage.

53

"Do you live around here?"

"Not really, I live in Huntington Beach. How about you?"

"Dallas. Let's do a lightning round."

"Lightning round?"

"Yeah. Three quick personal questions, one at a time, and you have to answer quickly. What's your favorite color?"

"Blue. Yours?"

"Pink. Your favorite meal?"

"Surf & Turf. Yours?"

"Lobster.

 Your greatest fear?"

"Deep water. Yours?"

"Heights. That's an interesting greatest fear; did you have an experience?"

"As a kid, I was on my surfboard at Rosarita Beach in Mexico. I got pulled out to deep water by a riptide, and looked below me and saw an Orca, a killer whale. The sunlight hit at such an angle that I could see how deep the water was, and the immense size of the whale. Took me 20 minutes, and all my strength, to get back to shore…"

Chapter 14

Wendy Gilbert's radar gave her sufficient indication that Jake had not alerted to her cocaine induced condition, and that it would be safe to ride with him to Perq's bar at the Huntington Beach pier. However, her own intoxication was more profound than she had realized. As she rose from the bar stool, her legs felt numb, but she could still maintain a reasonable degree of stability to walk from the bar, past the pool, and into the parking lot. She had told Karla where she would be going, since Karla elected to stay at the hotel. But her new co-worker felt obligated to at least follow them a short distance to ensure that she saw Wendy made it to Jake's Range Rover.

Jake suggested they first visit the "coolest place at night to watch the planes landing," before heading up to Pacific Coast Highway toward Huntington Beach. The scenic spot was a small parking structure on Main Street, west of MacArthur. The top level had no cover, and was in direct line with the final approach to John Wayne Airport's main runway. Few vehicles remained on the structure, since it served the businesses primarily working daytime operations. As the jets would descend before crossing the 405 Freeway, the engine roar would suddenly be deafening for a moment before touch down.

After the third flyover, Jake slowly moved his arm over Wendy's shoulders, and drew closer, placing his lips against Wendy's, tasting her lip gloss. She kissed back gently, but felt the right spaghetti strap on her dress move off her shoulder, as it was guided by Jake's hand past her bicep. Wendy was drunk, but her intoxication had not reached the point of losing control, so she reached her arm across her chest, and grabbed Jake's hand to prevent any further advancement of her dress past her bust line. Wendy's mind then began to race,

"This is way too fast!

This is not how cops are supposed to act!

Who is this? I've got to get out!"

The mixture of anabolic steroid with alcohol instantly pushed Jake's demeanor to rage, as he ripped the strap to her waist, exposing her breasts. Wendy screamed as she turned her back to Jake, and reached into her purse on the floor, retrieving a rattail comb with her left hand. In an arcing backhand motion, she swung the pointed end of the comb into his hip, piercing the pants and causing a deep puncture into the skin. Reflexively, he drove a hammer fist into the base of her neck, and she went silent.

Wendy lay sideways and unconscious on the passenger seat, with her head resting on the passenger door armrest. She was breathing slowly, and her dress, hiked up to her waist, exposed her pink panties. Jake faced sideways toward Wendy, and was wedged between the steering wheel and the driver's seat. He stared, fixated on her backside as his hip throbbed and bled. He unbuckled his blue jeans to check his wound, and saw that the blood wasn't pumping, or draining profusely. He pulled a bandana from his jacket pocket and tied it around his hip, and then looked again toward Wendy's panties.

Jake knew that he should be aroused, but the combination of the drug, alcohol, and pain left him with no feeling other than a sense of anger and fear over what he was going to do with the predicament confronting him. Attempted rape and assault meant prison, loss of job, reputation shattered. He had been here before, where the reality had failed to go according to the fantasy. He reached down and lifted his pant leg, exposing the small caliber, semi-automatic pistol in a holster on his ankle. He unsnapped the thumb break, and withdrew the weapon. Pointing it at the base of her skull, he fired one round. Wendy Gilbert had breathed her last breath.

~

The Range Rover lumbered down Old Barranca Road, the headlights illuminating the landmark, but its driver was focused solely on traffic. If anyone else elected to share the road, he'd have to eliminate the location. This ultimate criminal act required solitude. It could not survive a witness, and Jake's experience told him that the next steps in preventing discovery would be meaningless if someone saw his Rover at the tree.

No headlights approached, and a quick glance at the mirrors gave no indication that Jake's car was sharing the road with anyone. The full moon, however, was problematic. Its light reflected down onto the asparagus fields and the roadway, but cast the tree's shadow toward the freeway. This would leave the Rover exposed, without a temporary blanket of darkness that a few hours difference could provide. He had to be quick, but smooth.

He pulled the Rover to the right, onto the dirt shoulder and slowed to a stop parallel to the tree. He exited the driver's door, rounded the tailgate, and then opened the passenger door. Wendy's lifeless body rolled sideways, halfway out of the car. He grabbed her arms, dragged her the rest of the way out and across the shoulder to the base of the tree, deep into the low hanging foliage. He dropped her, lying face up, with her cocktail dress covering only one breast and her midsection. He then quickly walked back to the vehicle, shuffling his feet to disrupt any patterns of sole prints left by his shoes.

He backed the Rover up over its tracks, and suddenly accelerated, throwing dust and rocks in all directions, leaving no tire impression other than an unidentifiable skid mark tracing from dirt to weathered asphalt. Jake headed southbound toward

Sand Canyon, and then turned left toward Interstate 5, constantly checking his mirrors until merging into evening traffic.

He never considered his actions pathology. It was simply himself acting out what he desired. The narcissist in him felt normal. It was her fault that she had overreacted, as had others. Someone else would clean up his mess, and that would be the end of it.

Chapter 15

Hunter could hardly contain his excitement after ending his phone conversation with Tom Blackburn. They finally had a clue, workable information on a serial homicide suspect. A silver Range Rover, the description provided by Karla, who reported her co-worker missing this morning, was the piece of the puzzle that would jump start the investigative machine. The small caliber bullet hole would link the two crimes, but that British SUV, which signified status, would give them hope that they could accomplish an arrest and a conviction.

Hunter convened the team of six investigators at the station who were assigned to the cases, including Blackburn and Miller. Conference room white boards on the walls displayed the evidence and the profiles of Kimberly Donahue and Wendy Gilbert. The wall on the right, listed the Donahue homicide. On the left, across the conference table, Blackburn was finishing the bullet points on the whiteboard with his black felt-tip pen for the Gilbert homicide.

"We need to get a clean photo of a silver Range Rover that looks like Karla Bergstrom's description, and send it out on a flyer to all Orange and LA County agencies." Hunter opened.

"She was pretty traumatized, and only saw the driver's side and the backside of the car in the dark," Blackburn replied.

"Did she remember any of the letters or numbers of the plate? Actually, did she remember if there was even a visible license plate?"

"She remembered that the Rover had California colored plates, but could not remember any of the letters or numbers. Under the lights of the parking lot, she was pretty sure the color was silver, and that it appeared to be a later model, but does not remember seeing a license plate frame."

"OK, that's good. The models don't change that much. I think we have enough to put together a flyer. I think we might want to consider checking car rental agencies also. Miller can you pull an auto theft detective, someone familiar with car models, to team up with our homicide team?"

"I can handle that, Lieutenant. I worked GTA (grand theft auto) for three years before my assignment to robbery/homicide. Remember?" Stephanie Winslow replied.

Detective Stephanie Winslow could best be described as having a "Type A" personality, with an abundance of energy. Athletic, with a classic runner's frame, she was outstanding on multiple levels of performance, ranging from resourcefulness to maintaining of perishable skills, such as firearms proficiency.

"Thanks Steph, can you get started on that flyer? Then check the rental agencies at John Wayne Airport and Long Beach Municipal for starters. Thanks."

"No problem."

"Hey Tom, the second victim's co-worker, Karla, said the suspect claimed to the victim that he was a cop, but you said that she could not remember if he identified an agency. Do you know if either she or the victim were convinced?"

"She said the lack of facial hair, the short haircut, how he was dressed, and his manner of speech, was similar to police or military. But she also said that the victim was pretty high on cocaine, and thought it was rather obvious. She said she didn't think a cop would want to hang out with a coke user."

"OK, see if you can get Karla to go with you to Huntington Beach PD, and see if that gal that does the suspect sketches can get a drawing from her description. Since they were supposedly heading to the Huntington Beach pier, you might ask the artist if her sketch resembles anyone she might recognize from her department or any other. We've got small caliber, possibly .25 auto, for both homicides, and the tree. Is there any other similar criteria for the Crime Analysis Unit?" Hunter inquired.

"They both occurred on Fridays," Blackburn replied.

Chapter 16

"Aunt Erin, I listed you again as a reference for another background check. Is that OK?"

"Of course Alex, but didn't we just go through that? It seems as though you had passed through that inquisition so recently. Must we endure this again?"

"It's a different department Aunt Erin. It's Long Beach, and the Sheriff's Department is taking too long to put me on patrol."

"Can't Uncle Daniel take care of that for you? Can't he just call the Sheriff and get their background check from him? He is the chief of police for the City of Long Beach, for goodness sake."

"I haven't told him yet. I wanted to get as far through the process as I could on my own. Our last names are different; I'll play that card only if I have to."

"I'm lecturing at a conference in Vegas soon; hopefully they'll contact me when I return."

Dr. Erin O'Connell, Alex Vannover's aunt, was considered his closest relative, and he regarded her with the utmost respect. She was well aware of her sister's neglect in raising him, and the cold, authoritarian discipline practiced by his detached father.

Life in the Vannover home was focused on career and social status. Daniel suffered an upbringing that his aunt was certain would lead to delinquency, so she stepped in, filling a void created by his mom's inattention, to hopefully be that change agent in his life.

The busy surgeon attended his Little League games, took photos of Alex with his homecoming dance dates, but more importantly, offered encouragement instead of criticism. Although her career afforded no time to raise a family of her own,

Erin O'Connell made accommodation for Alex, ensuring that there was always a place for him at her home.

~

Scott Hunter had extensive training and experience with a particularly difficult criminal to identify and apprehend – the psychopath. As a graduate of the FBI's prestigious National Academy, Hunter studied profiling these individuals and the victimology associated with them.

He drove down Alton Parkway, heading for a lunch date with Ashley, and pondered the two homicides, looking for similarities and potential signs of the perpetrator's psychopathy. The dumping of their bodies in such a manner, under a lone tree next to a nearly forgotten road, demonstrated a complete detachment from the victims' humanity. The fact that others choosing this method of disposal, had been deemed psychopaths, added weight to this suspect's diagnosis.

His cool indifference to them by the exposure of their private parts or undergarments reflected an absolute callousness. The steps employed avoiding detection, such as the very location selected, and the defacing of footprints, revealed a consciousness of criminality, but not necessarily guilt.

Hunter wondered how these girls had let their guards down. Was it the drugs or alcohol? What qualities about the suspect lured them into a place of vulnerability? Their backgrounds interacting with men should have alerted them to danger.

But Hunter knew psychopaths are extremely manipulative. They view their victims as prey, and use charm in a cold-blooded way to achieve their goals. This guy was probably glib and charming, and would even seek to control an inexperienced detective trying to interrogate him.

Hunter arrived at Maizuru, his favorite Japanese restaurant. Located within the upscale Gelson's market shopping center, it provided a quiet, private place to enjoy a meal and good company. Ashley hadn't arrived yet, so he was seated at a secluded table toward the back, where he took notes while awaiting her arrival.

It was her day off, so she had ample time to prepare. Working different shifts and hours, gave them little time for intimacy, so she would make this rare moment special. As she opened the restaurant door, the wind carried the faint scent of her perfume immediately to Hunter's table, announcing her arrival. Although every male in the restaurant noticed her entrance, Ashley's smile radiated to the only person mattering to her, the square-jawed cop in the back corner whose eyes widened as he rose to greet her.

The sun shining through the glass door behind her, framed the outline of the tawny brunette drawing closer to his table. The lines of her white blouse with a plunging neckline were tastefully complemented with a single strand of pearls. Her pastel coral skirt ended just above the knees, revealing sculpted legs, elegantly matched with a pair of spiked heels. Ashley was breathtaking. Hunter knew that she was the one, and he was speechless.

As they embraced, Ashley gave him a peck on his cheek, and he blushed, while whispering, "I love you" in her ear.

"You look beautiful sweetheart." "You're pretty GQ yourself, mister, in your blue blazer and your pleated, khaki chinos. So, how many times have you saved the world today, my love?"

"None so far, but we've finally got a vehicle to look for, and a composite drawing of the suspect in our second pepper tree homicide."

"Really? Well that's sure welcome news!"

"These are tough cases to investigate, and just as challenging to avoid personalizing them."

Changing the subject, Ashley said, "Let's talk about our next vacation,"

When the meal ended, Hunter stood and adjusted Ashley's chair as she rose. Behind their table a beaded curtain separated a secluded room for private group events. Hunter parted the beads with his hand, and gently guided Ashley inside. As her eyes rose to his, Hunter's lips passionately met Ashley's, and his arms enveloped her waist and shoulders. This moment of discreet intimacy gave her all the assurance she needed that he was hers.

Chapter 17

Senior Police Officer Robert "Bob" Luther was assigned to the Long Beach Police Department's Training Division, and coordinated the background investigations of police recruits and lateral transfers. His day began as they normally started, reviewing the list of experienced officers from other departments seeking employment at Long Beach. Before checking the recruit roster for the next academy, Luther took a second gulp of coffee, and pulled the background package with a name he recognized from the lateral list.

Luther's brother, Dave, was a deputy with the Orange County Sheriff's Department, and had warned him about a guy working as a special deputy at the airport, who boasted about his uncle being the chief of police for Long Beach. The chief's name was Steinhoffer, but the nephew's last name was Vannover.

Luther took this assignment seriously, and felt personal responsibility for ensuring that every applicant receiving his recommendation for hire reflected the department's values. He opened the cover, and began reading the summary sheet prepared by the investigating officer. What drew his attention were the comments pertaining to character:

"...in the one year of his employment as a Special Deputy assigned to the airport, the Sheriff's Department has received two complaints by young women alleging that the applicant has verbally communicated an interest in dating them. The complaints were investigated at the supervisory level, rather than by Internal Affairs, and were sustained as violations of departmental policy. The first reported occurrence resulted in a letter of reprimand, and the second incident's punishment recommendation was two days suspension without pay. Under an appeal to his commanding officer, the punishment was reduced to a one day suspension."

Luther made one call to the Sheriff's Department for additional details, and then attached his recommendation sheet to the cover of the package. It said: "No Hire – See Character Narrative." He would normally send it along to the chief's office, but since the chief would have a personal interest in the applicant, Luther elected to hand carry it in to him for discussion. Steinhoffer was out of town; the meeting would have to wait until tomorrow.

~

"I got a letter today from American Airlines!"

"Good news?"

"Yes! They've given me a conditional notice of hire," Ashley announced, while gasping for air from excitement.

"And what are the conditions for hire?" Hunter inquired pragmatically.

"Passing their training program – you don't sound very excited."

"Sweetheart, it's bittersweet. I'm extremely happy for you, but I'll miss having you here at the department. I'm also worried that our time together will dramatically decrease, as you work the hours of a rookie flight attendant.

However, of course we need to celebrate. Let's plan a dinner at the Chart House."

"It'll work out; we'll be fine. Chart House sounds great. Love you."

~

It was just another spinal fusion, one of the roughly 300 performed by Dr. Erin O'Connell each year. But today she was particularly exhausted by lack of sleep. She was hoping her crankiness was the only visible symptom. She knew that

68

something must be done to address the vandalism occurring on her neighbor's property. Last night, it was a cherry bomb to their mailbox, and the week before, it had been a loud toilet papering.

She had spoken to the Prescott family about a month ago, when their teenage daughter, who seemed to be the likely target for all this had a sleepover interrupted by a drive-by water ballooning. Sally Prescott was a very understanding neighbor, and was supportive of Erin's efforts to have her husband assign officers to the problem.

Usually, Erin could vent to Daniel and he would quickly take care of the matter; but now his influence and attention were in Long Beach.

Erin & Daniel's Shady Canyon home was huge, even by Irvine standards. The gate-guarded community was exclusive, with well paid, conscientious guards. The real issue was the neighborhood kids. They drove BMW's purchased by their doting parents, texted incessantly during their classes, and considered challenging authority a contact sport. Erin would have to reconnect with Sally Prescott and ask that she take proactive measures to prevent another occurrence, or else a future surgical procedure could have a tragic outcome.

Chapter 18

Bob Luther sat in one of two chairs facing Chief Steinhoffer's expansive teak desk, and he was sweating. While awaiting the end of Steinhoffer's phone conversation with the Sheriff, his mind ran through various scenarios in support of his recommendation that the Chief's nephew not be hired. He feared that this discussion would soon become confrontational. This chief's philosophy of participative management was, "I manage; you participate." The portly, 5'8" pit bull held little patience for contrary opinions, and showed minimal regard for traditions. Change was a constant in the departments he managed, and simply relying on past practices was a losing tactic for justifying decisions made.

The closing salutations were being given and the battle was about to commence.

"Well Bob, I read your recommendation, and I think you need to do a little more work on this."

"Sir?"

"The background investigation regarding my nephew allegedly asking women for dates while on-duty doesn't address the credibility of the complainants."

"Sir, I spoke with the Sheriff's Department sergeant who investigated the complaints, and each complainant emphatically stated that they wished to remain anonymous."

"Well, there you have it. Their veracity cannot be determined, so as far as I'm concerned, it is as if these events never happened."

"But Chief, we've encountered similar complaints within our own organization, and have interviewed complainants thoroughly to determine their credibility. We could still make judgments as to the accuracy of their allegations, without having to disclose their identities."

"There you go again, with your reliance on "how we've always done it in the past." My belief is that people complaining behind the cloak of anonymity cannot be trusted."

"Sir, he-said / she-said complaints are extremely difficult, and when you add in the factor of the male party being a police officer, it takes a huge amount of courage to file a complaint. These women are understandably fearful of retaliation."

"Nonsense! I refuse to accept anonymous slander to deny someone a career. Send him a notice of intent to hire, and schedule him a physical."

"Chief, I understand the sensitivity of this issue, since it involves your nephew, but I think we should give him at least another year with his current agency, to ensure that we are not inheriting someone else's problem."

"I can recognize faulty investigative work when I see it. I have spoken all that I care to on this matter. You have your orders on the disposition of this applicant's package. Take care of it."

~

Blackburn finally caught up with the bartender who had worked at the Airporter Hotel's lounge the evening Wendy Gilbert had been killed. Tom Hunsaker had been tending bar there for a little over three years, and remembered "Jake," from the night of the homicide.

"Had you seen the subject we'll refer to as "Jake" before the night that Wendy Gilbert was killed?" Blackburn asked, after describing the man with whom Gilbert was last seen leaving.

"Quite frankly, I hadn't seen the guy before that night. But there are a lot of non-regulars visiting this lounge. The hotel is across the street from the airport, and a percentage of the patrons stay the night, and catch a flight the next day to their ultimate destination."

"Do you remember what he ordered to drink?"

"He was drinking Coors Lite."

"Did you engage in conversation?"

"Not much, mostly small talk. I had a high school football game on the TV, and he seemed pretty interested in the game."

"Do you remember the teams that were playing that night?"

"Mater Dei and I think it was Bishop Amat."

"Did he show an interest in one team over the other?"

"Mater Dei, but as you probably know, that's a popular team in Orange County. But, he could have played linebacker there, he was about the size and build of a high school linebacker."

"Did he use a credit or debit card to pay for his drinks?"

"As I recall, he paid cash."

"The victim's co-worker said that he looked like he was police or military. Do you think that's an accurate description?"

"Yeah, he had short brown hair, but not buzz cut, like a Marine. He was more like a military pilot, or maybe local police. His hair was parted, like yours."

"Did he have any jewelry, like a ring or a watch with a service insignia?"

"Not that I can remember."

"What about tattoos?"

"Nothing visible."

"Did you see them leave together? Can you recall their condition?"

"You could tell she was definitely feeling a little tipsy, but not so affected that we wouldn't serve her. He was fine; provided support around her waist. But I don't think she really needed it. It was more affection, probably hoping he'd get lucky. How'd he kill her?"

"Well, we're waiting for the final autopsy report from the coroner." Blackburn stalled.

"I thought she was really pretty, and a bubbly personality from what I could tell."

"Not anymore."

~

Sgt. Keith Miller and Detective Stephanie Winslow walked into the detective bureau, each carrying banker's boxes of paperwork collected from their search warrant service at the outcall agency. Typical of such businesses, the Sheffield Escort Agency kept minimal documentation on the girls who were sent on "dates," culminating in sex. Upon reaching Hunter's office, Miller stopped and shared their preliminary findings.

"Hey boss, not much help at the escort service."

"Not much assistance, or nothing really useful?"

"Well, actually both, as expected. The girls all provide a fictitious name, and the name associated with our victim's phone number was "Tiffany Huxley." The day of the murder, they recorded a scheduled "date" with a "Jake Johnson," and a meeting location at Turk's restaurant in Dana Point Harbor."

"Did they check his call back number?"

"The manager said they always do. We just called it, and it was disconnected."

"Do the records show that the call was received the same day that the escort service was to take place?"

"Can't tell, they just entered the date of the service."

"OK, how long do they keep their client records?"

"Well, she said one year. We'll be going through these files in the conference room to see if his name or number shows up again."

"Why don't you head down to Turk's and see if anyone remembers our victim. You can check the files later; the names and numbers are probably bogus."

Chapter 19

Chief Steinhoffer sat impatiently in the back booth of the Chinese restaurant waiting for his usual lunch date with his boss, City Manager Suzanne Duncan. The normal discussion of business and romance would have an added attraction: an investment opportunity that could be extremely profitable.

Steinhoffer knew that terminating pursuits had continued to be problematic. In earlier times, a shotgun round to the tires was sufficient to achieve rapid deflation, but controlling the rapid deceleration became a dangerous result. Another way to stop a vehicle was The Police Intervention Tactic or the "PIT maneuver" in which the police cruiser's front bumper would strike the suspect vehicle's rear bumper at an angle causing it to spin to a halt. But it could only be performed at lower speeds, and required significant hours of training.

Steinhoffer was counting on the fact that most law enforcement agencies had begun to use spike strips to cause a more controlled deflation of the suspect vehicle's tires, even though deployment of the strips had resulted in several workers compensation claims for puncture wounds to the officers' hands during deployment.

Still, Steinhoffer was certain that he could convince Duncan of the need for the country to begin using the strips. And, as a bonus, he could talk her into using his friend's company that was producing prototypes of spike strips that would stop the pursuits, as well as the accompanying injuries.

Since use of the strips would need testing, clearly his department would be an excellent choice to be the beta site. If or when the tests were found to be successful, then investors in this device's production, coincidentally like him, would stand to gain significant profits.

The restaurant for this meeting had become part of the fabric of Long Beach's upscale district known as Bixby Knolls. Lee Yen's had been a fixture on Atlantic Avenue for several years, and had developed a steady patronage of locals who wanted a good Chinese lunch or dinner at a reasonable price.

Steinhoffer's stomach growled at the aroma of fried rice sizzling in the wok. He looked up from his notepad. Suzanne Duncan's arrival was always a statement. Her striking appearance, almost military posture, and assertive gait caught the attention of every patron, cook, and waitress in the establishment. If this was to be a quiet, discreet meeting; that opportunity passed the moment Ms. Duncan ventured into Lee Yen's.

"Suzanne, you are a vision!"

"Cut the sucking up, Daniel. You'd say that if I looked hung over."

"Look, I get the rank structure. The chief of police reports to the city manager, but I really care for you, and I have since Irvine."

"That's sweet Daniel, have you ordered my iced tea?"

"Yes, where's our waitress? She should have brought it to our table by now."

"Well, what is it that got you so excited on the phone? Another DOJ grant?"

"No, do you remember my telling you about Ruben Cohen?"

"Not really, refresh my memory."

"Reuben owns a research and development company, which is a defense contractor. They build modifications and enhancements to existing firearms in the military, and he has branched out with a division that's producing police equipment. He's developed a prototype for a new pursuit terminating spike strip."

76

"So are you asking me for a budget increase to buy some?"

"No! I'm talking about investing in his company and making a small fortune when his product not only ends pursuits, but stops all these workers comp claims for spikes that puncture our officers' hands."

"What's he looking at for an initial investment?"

"Well, I'm providing him with technical advice, so he's only asking for $75,000 spread among three investors, for a 30% stake, or 10% for each investor."

"Who's the third investor?"

"His brother."

"What does his brother do for a living?"

"He's an anesthesiologist."

"What's so special about his product?"

"The officer doesn't use two hands to throw the spikes. He uncovers them. They're attached to a rigid cable, wrapped in a plastic cover, and attached to a toggle switch. The officer pushes them out into the traffic lane, holds the toggle switch in one hand, and pushes the handle forward with the other hand, causing the spikes to rise from a horizontal position to vertical. The suspect's vehicle passes over them, tires are punctured, and the officer pulls the handle back, causing the spikes to return to the horizontal position. He pulls the spike strips back, covers them, and puts them back into his trunk."

"Does your friend have any experience in police equipment development, financing, and marketing?"

"He's got years of experience in dealing with this same type of thing at the federal level."

"OK, but military equipment is a whole different development, and the marketing is much more restricted."

"Well, we'll test them out with a couple of our officers, run a few clunker cars over the device, and videotape the tests for a marketing company."

"Wait a minute, we're going to be investors, and we're going to use City resources to test a product in which we have a vested interest?"

"The spikes have to be tested. Our department has the equipment to conduct a valid test. This is done all the time. Are we going to ask LAPD to test them, and showcase their department?"

"Daniel, I don't like giving them any more attention than they already receive from Hollywood. But the appearances are problematic."

"All right, I can see that you're uncomfortable with this proposition. I think we're fine, but I'm not going to put any pressure on you. Let's just see how things develop in the R & D stages and leave it alone for now."

"Daniel, I think you need to be careful with this and stay away from any appearance of impropriety."

Chapter 20

It was Monday evening, and John Wayne Airport was the scheduled venue for the next quarterly JHAT (Joint Hazardous Assessment Team) training evolution. At 10:30 PM, the site was chilly, but the clear sky overhead sparkled with the expanse of stars, despite the hotel lights illuminating MacArthur Boulevard. The airport officially closed at 11:00 PM, and re-opened at 7:00 AM giving Orange County's elite counter-terrorist team the graveyard shift to practice aircraft entries.

A Southwest Airlines 737 was made available to choreograph the fields of fire within the fuselage, leading up to speed drills for adversary takedowns, and controlling of hostages. The lines of armored vehicles, including BEARS, BEARCATS, and Suburbans arrived at the upper level for departures. Teams lined up by agency: Anaheim PD, Huntington Beach PD, Irvine PD, Orange County Sheriff's Department, and Santa Ana PD, with ten - operators each. These were the top officers within their respective teams, and received the best equipment for the most challenging missions.

Once the teams deployed into the terminal, their vehicles needed security, so a small cadre of Sheriff's Department Special Deputies were assigned an overtime detail guarding around fifteen vehicles. Alex Vannover was one of the fortunate few to receive this plumb assignment, but was running late. He needed to get into his uniform, but his Chevrolet pickup truck was still a block away from the airport entrance.

He parked his truck, ran to his locker, and saw that the other four deputies working with him had already deployed to the upper level. He emptied his pockets, and unwrapped his ankle holster containing his .25 auto, then placed it on the bench. Staring into his locker, he decided he wanted to look sharp standing next to these JHAT meat eaters, so he elected to put shirt suspenders on, to maintain the sharp creases in his shirt. He snapped one of the suspender ends to the bottom of his shirt, and the other ends at the top of his socks. He then pulled his trousers on, and tied his shoes. The Sam Browne gun belt was next, and he was ready to go. Upon exiting the locker room, he passed Special Deputy Larry Giroux, who was entering.

"What'd you forget?" Vannover asked.

"Cellphone! I'll be right back!"

"Copy."

Giroux arrived at his locker, retrieved the phone, and then turned toward the door. Just as he was leaving, he saw the outline of a small holstered pistol lying on the bench. He froze in total dismay. From his academy days, he recognized that an unattended firearm could be grounds for dismissal. His 6'3" hulking frame stood, hovering over the bench. His eyes widened, and his forehead wrinkled up to his blond crew cut.

He was shocked at the carelessness, but then remembered it was just last year that he was checking the charge on his Taser only to discover that it was still loaded with a cartridge. The explosion and subsequent burst of two darts missed his head, but smashed into the fluorescent light above, raining glass shards all over his co-workers below. That lapse in attention cost him a day's suspension without pay.

Giroux wasn't sure whose pistol lay on the bench before him, but suspected it belonged to Vannover. He was late, and was the last one in the room. Giroux paused to think. He could easily call Dispatch and have them run the serial number to determine its owner, but that could result in discipline for his fellow deputy. Or, he could simply wrap the weapon in a towel, take it to

Vannover, and if it was not his, he would resort to option number one.

He rode the escalator up to the arrival level, and walked along the row of armored vehicles, scanning for Vannover among the few remaining JHAT operators and Special Deputies milling around the BEARs. A green flash of light bolted across MacArthur Boulevard and landed on the front of the Hilton Hotel, approximately five (5) stories up. Giroux followed it back to its source, and found Vannover standing next to an Irvine officer pointing his M-4 carbine at the structure, demonstrating his new weapon- mounted green laser.

Giroux walked over to Vannover, marveling at the cool technology on display, and tapped him on the elbow, motioning for him to join him at the Sky Cap station.

"Alex, is this yours?"

Giroux discreetly unwrapped a towel, revealing the holstered pistol.

"Oh shit! Yeah, I must have left it on the bench."

"I figured it was yours. I've got a Beretta Jet Fire .25 just like it. They're easy to conceal, but not much knock down power. Better than nothing, though. Man, you gotta be more careful. If the Sarge had found it; you'd be toast."

"Thanks Larry; I owe you one."

"Ham and eggs is good. Across the street at I-Hop?"

Chapter 21

JHAT training finished early when the aircraft was called into service due to a mechanical problem in Oakland. Vannover and Giroux finished breakfast at I-Hop, with Vannover leaving both the tip, and paying the tab at the cash register. He considered it a small price to pay in comparison to what awaited him for his firearm indiscretion. As they walked into the parking lot their conversation continued.

"How were those ham and eggs?" Vannover inquired sheepishly.

"Pretty good, my favorite breakfasts are at the Dana Point Harbor. There's a place on the water that's kind of a dive, but it's pretty well known for fish and chips, and they serve breakfast for the fishermen before they go out in the morning."

"What are they called?"

"Umm...Turk's."

"I'll have to check them out. Thanks again man, for finding my gun. Is this your car?"

"Yeah, Land Rover Discovery. I snowboard in Mammoth a lot, and the four-wheel-drive on this is awesome. And I like the paint finish; it doesn't fade like the Toyota's and Honda's."

"The silver finish is pretty cool, and I like your 5-spoke wheels."

"Thanks."

"You live around Dana Point?"

"San Clemente, it's a bit of a drive to work, but I like surfing Trestles."

"You surf Trestles? I surf from Trestles to the Huntington Cliffs. We should go out when the surf's up, and maybe catch some fish and chips at your Dana Point dive."

"Sounds good."

~

Vannover's Chevy Silverado left the pancake house parking lot onto Business Center Drive, and stopped at MacArthur Boulevard, waiting for the through traffic to clear. A British racing green Ford Crown Victoria caught his attention as it passed and entered the northbound on-ramp to the 405 Freeway. It looked like the standard police staff car driven by detectives and command officers. In fact, it appeared to be his uncle's car, issued by Long Beach PD. Vannover followed, since the direction of travel also led to his Costa Mesa apartment.

He caught up to the Ford as they approached the 55 Freeway, and confirmed that it was his uncle, Chief Steinhoffer, driving the staff car. Vannover exited at Bristol, and Steinhoffer continued northbound, the direction he would normally take to reach the police station. Vannover was tired, following the graveyard shift and a heavy breakfast, but his mind couldn't shake his fixation on his uncle's course of travel.

The normal route from his home in Shady Canyon would be a straight shot up the 405 Freeway from Irvine to Long Beach. The 7:30 AM trek up MacArthur Boulevard from Newport Beach was puzzling. He knew that his aunt was away in Las Vegas, and thought it odd that his aunt's husband, as he preferred to call him, would be traveling through Newport Beach at that hour.

~

When he got back at his apartment, Vannover made a quick check at his mailbox, a practice reaching nearly obsessive levels since commencing his application process with Long Beach PD. This time there was an envelope bearing treasure. He was offered the job, and given a phone number to schedule his physical exam required for becoming a police officer with the City of Long Beach.

No longer would his days be filled with angry drivers refusing to follow the signs clearly posted curbside at the terminal. Perhaps an appointment to SWAT would be in his future, once he cleared probation. This was exciting, a future with a department that serviced a broad spectrum of communities, in a city that was hopping with challenging calls for service.

He then retrieved his cell phone from its holster to call the number for scheduling his physical, and noticed that a message had been left on his voicemail:

"Hi Alex, it's Aunt Erin. I received a call from the background investigator from the Long Beach Police Department a couple days ago, and he asked me the same type of questions that the Sheriff's detective asked me for your current job. He didn't need to meet with me, which was interesting. I guess since you were already with a law enforcement agency, a visit wasn't needed. Hopefully, you will hear from them soon. I'll be leaving here tonight. See you soon. Love you."

Chapter 22

Like most sophomores in high school, Amy Van der Linden was trying to fit in. The clothes and makeup she favored were Gothic, and her music preferences of Marilyn Manson, Alice Cooper, and Megadeath, tended to limit her circle of friends. Her sexually suggestive attire attracted the wrong group of interested males. Her parents were hoping this was a phase that would be short-lived.

Her walk home from El Toro High School seemed to be uneventful, until the white Ford Econoline van with surf racks, and the cute blonde surfer kid offered her a ride. But his youthful appearance and demeanor were deceptive. This twenty-four year old meth and sex addict was taking a giant leap into criminality. He knew the area, having worked several years as a gardener, tending the expansive Lake Forest homes constructed beneath the shade of eucalyptus trees.

This seemed like the perfect place to troll for young girls. Most of the kids walked home from Serrano Middle School, as did some from El Toro High, because the neighborhoods were considered safe. He also blended in. If the high school guys weren't riding to the beach in vans or VW bugs, they were standing at bus stops holding surfboards.

Getting into his van, Amy was thinking boyfriend potential, but his mind was focused upon conquest and sexual relief. His suggestion of Baskin Robbins sounded like fun, but their direction of travel didn't seem to be heading toward any ice cream parlor with which she was familiar. He said that his name was "Trevor," but she had never seen him before, and he looked older up close, than her first impression from the sidewalk. She was beginning to think accepting this ride might not be such a good idea after all.

Her concern grew when she saw that Trevor's exit from the freeway at Sand Canyon was devoid of any homes or businesses, and agricultural fields and a dusty road were the only scenery visible for a couple miles. When they passed a lonely roadside tree she became really frightened and asked where they were going.

Trevor's response was only, "Shut up, we're almost there."

The van crossed Jeffrey Road, and reached a dead end at a rock quarry, where Trevor stopped and turned the ignition key off. This place was completely deserted. There were no structures or vehicles anywhere around the piles of rocks stacked adjacent to a large, concrete flood control channel.

Trevor immediately sprung from his driver's seat onto Amy, plunging his tongue through her lips, and down her throat. She struggled to push him off her, but fell between the seats, as he tore her black mesh stockings down her legs, followed by her panties, which he pulled down, below her black skirt. She screamed as he entered her, but his hand covered her mouth, as the full weight of his body came down, pinning her to the floor.

The vicious attack only lasted a few seconds and ended with Trevor punching her twice in the jaw, causing her to nearly lose consciousness. He quickly left the van, opened the back doors, then grabbed her arms and began pulling her out. Amy struggled to stay awake, but the last thing she saw was the tattoo on his forearm of wings and a sentence starting with the word "Bury" and ending with "Harley."

Trevor dragged her body behind a stacked pile of rocks, lifted a large boulder overhead, and dropped it onto her head, hoping to eliminate the only witness to his crime. His van left the quarry, heading south on Jeffrey Road, and disappeared into the southbound lanes of the 405 Freeway.

Dr. Peter Kim, Professor of Biology at the University of California, Irvine, would have been the last person to have thought that his act of forgetfulness could be considered fortuitous. His moment of distraction resulted in his placing the envelope containing his vehicle registration in the glove box of his Hyundai Santa Fe, without first removing the registration tabs, and placing them on the vehicle's license plate. Instead of his sedan displaying current registration, its obvious delinquent status caught the attention of Sgt. Richard Austin, who was working the swing shift on Tuesday, at 4:15 PM in the area of Jeffrey Road and Old Barranca Road. Austin turned on his lights and initiated a car stop.

As Dr. Kim's presentation of the current tabs, and the subsequent warning given by Sgt. Austin ended the contact, they both looked ahead toward the rock quarry, and were incredulous at the sight of a partially nude teenage girl with a bloody face staggering toward them. Amy van der Linden collapsed into the arms of the department's senior-most supervisor.

Chapter 23

Austin hit the emergency button on his radio, broadcasted the crime, and requested paramedics and backup. He grabbed a thermal blanket from the trunk, and wrapped it around Amy before laying her across the back seat of his cruiser. A portion of her forehead was crushed, but she was able to give Austin her name, followed by "El Toro High School," "white van," "blonde Trevor," and "Bury...Harley."

Hunter, who had been monitoring the radio traffic, ran to Sgt. Keith Miller's office and directed him to send Blackburn and Winslow out to the scene. Hunter then donned his windbreaker, and sped toward the rock quarry. He mentally went through a checklist of things that he needed to get rolling, without stepping on Austin, who had his hands full, as reflected in the flurry of radio transmissions.

Austin assigned an officer to ride with the victim to Mission Hospital Trauma Center, and a Crime Scene Investigation (CSI) team was sent from the station. To minimize radio traffic, Hunter phoned Dispatch, requesting they notify the Sheriff's Department to send an additional CSI team, and to contact the high school for the victim's emergency numbers to get her parents on their way to the hospital. Detective Winslow, stocked her briefcase with a rape kit, and drove a separate car to the hospital while Blackburn drove directly to the crime scene. He advised Winslow he would meet up with her at the hospital and would bring some crime scene photos to assist in any interviewing of the victim, once her condition was stabilized.

When Hunter arrived, he was briefed by Austin, while patrol officers deployed crime scene tape, and cordoned off a lane of traffic for police vehicles. In terms of physical evidence left at the scene, there was little to be collected other than the suspect's shoe prints, the van's tire treads, and blood deposited on the rocks.

The white van would contain a significant amount of evidence, but it would take a near miraculous car stop to retrieve it, based upon the limited description provided by the victim. Hunter's guess, however, was that the most compelling information incriminating this suspect would be found on the victim's body in the form of DNA from semen, fingernail scrapings, hair samples, and skurff, loose human cells transmitted from one body to another. Hunter knew these valuable cells were used by bloodhounds tracking the scents left by fleeing suspects.

Hunter followed a CSI technician who was snapping photos of the rock quarry from several positions in relation to Jeffrey Road and Old Barranca, making certain that his steps didn't contaminate the scene. Looking southbound down Old Barranca, his gaze fixed upon the familiar pepper tree, approximately half a mile away. He paused, while thinking about the many faces that had been left within close proximity to that landmark.

He now had another case number with a face that he needed to clear, but this time, he would hopefully have a live victim to help steer him toward an arrest. Perhaps this one could even help clear a few more.

~

Additional information regarding the van came from the ambulance as it was exiting Interstate 5 at Crown Valley Parkway. Amy was able to tell the officer seated next to her that the suspect's van was old and beat up in appearance, with a set of surf racks attached to the roof. Hunter decided this information, coupled with the suspect's tattoo, was sufficient to initiate a countywide broadcast, to enable all officers on duty within the County of Orange to look for a vehicle and suspect matching those descriptions, and to stake out predetermined freeway checkpoints for the next thirty minutes.

Since Hunter owned a Harley Davidson Sportster, he had collected a fair amount of the motorcycle company's memorabilia. While concentrating on the cryptic words furnished by the victim regarding the suspect's tattoo, he could think of no more likely phrase than "Bury Me with My Harley." It would be considered an entry level puzzle question for the TV show, "Wheel of Fortune," but critical in narrowing down a suspect.

He directed Dispatch to add it to the broadcast as a possible completion for the phrase. Before leaving the scene, Hunter approached one of the patrol officers preparing to return to service, and asked him to search within a one mile radius, subject to call, for another twenty minutes. Sometimes suspects return to the scene out of curiosity, and he wanted to cover that possibility.

The CSI teams worked until sundown casting tire treads and shoe impressions, after having collected blood specimens. The chill of the night fell upon the scene warranting the donning of field jackets, and sampling of Starbucks coffee delivered by Explorer Scouts eager to be useful. The normal flow of 50 mile per hour traffic slowed to a crawl in response to the amber flashing lights of the CSI utility trucks, and flood lights from the news vans capturing the requisite evening interview from the field.

~

Amy Van der Linden's stunned parents and sister arrived at the hospital just as Amy was entering the operating room for surgery. Mission Hospital Trauma Center rose above Interstate 5 atop a hill surrounded by medical offices, and an expansive, upscale mall curiously named "The Shops at Mission Viejo." The Trauma Center was the preferred destination for injured police and firefighters, based upon its reputation for having a stable of thoroughbred specialty surgeons, and a nursing staff that made certain their uniformed patients received care on a par with Nordstrom's.

Detective Winslow's Ford slowly wound up the road leading to the emergency room parking lot. Her thoughts drifted to her last visit here, when her niece had fought to survive following a fatal collision on Oso Parkway. She hoped that Amy's story would have a better ending.

Winslow was met at the nurse's station by a Hispanic ER nurse with a bright smile, and straight black hair with neatly trimmed bangs. Winslow handed her the rape kit, gave her directions, and then scanned the waiting room for the officer who had ridden in the ambulance with the victim. Spotting the Irvine uniform, she signaled the athletic rookie to follow her down the hallway to an empty clerical office. After audio-recording his statement, she located the Van der Linden family in the surgical waiting room.

Recalling her own hospital waiting room experience, she recognized her need to handle this encounter delicately. She smiled warmly, and following introductions, began to write down the names of friends and school staff that might have either seen her abduction, or knew of anyone who could possibly be responsible.

Back at the crime scene, Hunter directed Miller to apply his computer skills to create a flyer depicting a sketch of the van and the tattoo. He then notified the local TV stations that he would be giving a brief press conference for the 11:00 PM news. Blackburn had phoned the high school principal and made arrangements to visit the campus the next day to meet with students, teachers, and staff to re-trace the victim's steps prior to the crime.

Winslow would remain at the hospital to await the completion of Amy's surgery, and the arrival of Blackburn. She sat taking notes, surrounded by antiseptic odors, beeping sounds of medical equipment, and family members weeping in response to the unthinkable.

Chapter 24

For twenty minutes Officer Jim Janowitz had one mission – find an older model white van with surf racks. He limited his grid pattern to Old Barranca Road, Sand Canyon Road, Irvine Center Drive, and Jeffrey Road. For him, the purpose for which he had been assigned was unique. He would be looking for a suspect who might be returning to the scene of a crime. It sounded like something out of Sherlock Holmes, and yet he had learned about this behavior in the class he'd taken in preparation for the detective's test.

Janowitz turned his patrol car onto westbound Old Barranca Road, heading toward the very spot where, just weeks prior, he had found his first body dump. The sudden flicker of brake lights startled him, and prompted the keying of his radio mic to announce his location. He held off hitting his high beams and light bar until he was close, giving little reaction time for the vehicle's occupants.

It was not the van to which he was assigned, but still, the silver Land Rover warranted a check. As he "lit them up" with light bar, spotlights, and high beams, he heard unit 39-332's transmission that he was responding for backup from Irvine Center Drive and Sand Canyon. The silhouettes inside indicated a male driver and, female passenger. Both remained motionless in their seats. He exited, and made a driver's side approach, with flashlight in his left hand, and right hand resting on his .45, with the thumb break holster's safety disengaged.

Upon reaching the rear bumper, Janowitz lightly pressed the trunk lid, ensuring that the lid was latched, and then scanned the empty back seats for weapons and contraband. At his arrival at the open driver's window, his quick sweep of their hands with his light detected no immediate threats.

To Janowitz's surprise, the driver had laid open a wallet showing a driver's license on his left thigh, and an open badge case on the right thigh. The badge case displayed the six pointed star of the Orange County Sheriff's Department, and the position markings read, "Special Deputy," similar to those worn by the airport detail.

As Janowitz took in a breath to speak, he smelled no pot or alcohol, but recognized the fresh aroma emitted by a new vehicle. He smiled, cancelled his backup officer, and then greeted the couple.

"How's Station 18 (O.C. Sheriff) tonight?"

"Great, thanks!"

"Are you folks having any car trouble?"

"No, we just stopped for a moment to talk."

The driver retrieved the driver's license from his wallet, and handed it to Janowitz. The name displayed was Larry Giroux. Janowitz glanced toward his female passenger, and could now smell the mixture of her perfume with the leather and plastics of the interior. She was striking, with bright blonde hair feathered over her shoulders, and an obvious breast augmentation. He was curious, but wasn't sure how to ask.

"Dating?"

"Well, actually first date."

Janowitz thought, escort, maybe porn.

"You familiar with this location, Larry?"

"Not really, just saw it from the freeway."

"A few weeks ago, I found a homicide victim here. May have been an escort, or prostitute."

Janowitz shot another quick look toward Giroux's passenger for her reaction. She sat stoically expressionless.

98

"A few days later, we had another one dropped here. She was an American Airlines flight attendant. We're looking for a silver Range Rover associated with that one. That's what sort of drew my attention to your car, but they're different models. You guys get the flyer on that one?"

"Must have missed it..."

Anyway, this is kind of a creepy place, and I wouldn't stay here any longer."

"Nice meeting you Larry. I didn't get your name, Miss."

"Amber. Amber Morgan."

"Nice meeting you, Amber. Goodnight."

Walking back to his car, Janowitz sensed something was odd, but he couldn't put it together. He needed more information on the two murder cases, and would have to talk to Blackburn tomorrow to see if he could get some answers.

Chapter 25

It began as one of those crazy conversations over dinner at the Caspian restaurant. A romantic meal of Persian cuisine was planned by Hunter to make up for the manic schedule that had created days of separation from Ashley. She had begun her flight attendant training, but only her sister was available to listen to Ashley's challenges in passenger safety. Her phone calls to Minneapolis would have to suffice, while Hunter worked long hours coordinating the homicide cases, and their private time was put on hold.

Now, however, this moment of intimacy by candlelight would be enjoyed with the simple pleasure of talking and listening about each other's upbringing. The topic of relationships with the opposite sex had come up, and Ashley inquired as to Hunter's earliest experience of romance with a girl. Hunter uncomfortably shared that that momentous event took place at the Magic Kingdom, Disneyland.

Hunter recounted an evening, at the age of fifteen, with his best friend, Tom, who had just gotten his driver's license. They both traveled to Disneyland in Tom's parents' Dodge Charger, and ended up in Fantasyland. Hunter met a willowy, sixteen year old brunette, and Tom was introduced to her girlfriend. After the four of them rode the carousel, they ventured onto the Snow White and the Seven Dwarfs Ride, which was a car that winded through Snow White's adventures in the dark. Hunter confessed that he kissed the brunette once during the ride, but never saw her after that night.

Ashley provided a story as bland as Melba toast, about a high school date to a Bon Jovi concert that ended with a kiss on the doorstep. She told Hunter that she had an idea for their next date night, but told him that she would "be in charge."

~

Mission Hospital's on-call head trauma surgeon was quickly on site, and his surgical team addressed Amy's injuries with precision. A titanium plate was inserted to replace portions of her crushed skull, and her vital signs were stabilized. It was anticipated that her brain swelling would decrease over the next few days, and they would then assess the extent, if any, that her motor or cognitive functions had been impaired.

Blackburn and Winslow left the hospital, and would await a call from the medical staff assigned to Amy's care, to attempt a follow-up interview for any additional details that she might remember. As their staff cars wound down the road from the hospital, they headed toward Dana Point Harbor for breakfast at Turk's, and to hopefully interview a waitress who might have seen Kimberly Donahue's meeting with "Jake" the day of her murder.

The morning fog was beginning to dissipate, only to be replaced by the diesel exhaust from the fishing boats leaving their moorings at the harbor. The scent of fish caught the ocean breeze, announcing the start of a red tide, and gave Winslow a wave of nausea as she stepped from her car onto the damp asphalt of the parking lot. She was not a fan of seafood, and her empty stomach and lack of sleep made the shrimp and albacore odors even more intolerable. She hoped that the menu was simple, and that the standard eggs, hash browns, and juice would save her.

Blackburn met her at the sidewalk by the Wind & Sea restaurant, where they walked down to the boardwalk leading to Turk's. The windows to Turk's were cluttered with various articles of nautical memorabilia, along with chalkboards of dinner specials according to days of the week. They walked up the ramp leading to the entrance, and opened the door, unleashing a wave of traditional breakfast smells of coffee, maple syrup, and ham, giving Winslow hope that her meal would succeed in reviving her.

Once seated at their booth, Blackburn's attention was drawn from the menu to the TV set over the bar which was tuned to the morning news. Hunter's on-camera interview from last evening covering the rock quarry assault included Miller's example of an older model van with surf racks, and a set of Harley Davidson wings with the cryptic phrase.

"Looks like Miller did his computer magic with those clues."

"Yeah, maybe somebody will pay attention, and give us a call."

"You think Hunter will buy ice cream for the bureau? That's a pretty big "owe" for the television exposure."

"Nah, that's if <u>we</u> go on TV, not lieutenants."

"True, but I bet he'll still show up with Eskimo Pies or at least ice cream sandwiches."

Upon paying the check, Blackburn asked the manager if he could speak with the waitress serving the tables in the back section of the restaurant, while his waitress covered. He agreed to attend to her station, while Blackburn, Winslow, and waitress Jennifer (Ginny) Martinez stepped outside for a brief interview.

"Hi Ginny, you had mentioned on the phone that you believe that you served the victim in our homicide case. Let me show you her photo to refresh your memory. Does this picture look like the gal that you served?"

"Yes, I saw her picture on TV, and I remembered waiting on them; so I called your office."

"Thank you, we certainly appreciate you coming forward. We are obviously interested in the person she ate with. Did you see them enter the restaurant together?"

"Well no, I didn't see them enter, but I saw them both seated in my station together, and I took their order."

"OK, can you describe the man that was seated with her?"

"He was tall, muscular, in his twenties."

"How tall would you say he was?"

"Oh, I would say six feet one, six feet two."

"What color was his hair?"

"It was dark, I think brown."

"Do you recall, was his hair parted?"

"Yes, but I'm not sure what side. He sat facing the entrance, so I think the part was on my side, which would be right, but again, I'm not sure."

"Can you estimate his weight?"

"He was maybe one hundred ninety, two hundred pounds, I think."

"Did he have any facial hair?"

"No, I didn't see any."

"How about scars, marks, tattoos, or eyeglasses?"

"I don't remember seeing any."

"Did he have any distinctive clothing?"

"He had a polo type shirt, because you could see the muscles on his arms, like a weight lifter."

"Do you recall what they ordered to eat and drink?"

"I think they both ordered the most popular dish – fish & chips. I think he had a beer. But she had champagne, which is kind of rare here."

"Do you remember how the bill was paid?"

"He paid cash."

"You seem to have a pretty good recollection of them. What was your impression? Did it appear to be a date? Could you tell if their conversation was romantic?"

"He was good looking, she was very attractive – a lot of makeup. He was talking more, asking questions. I really couldn't hear much of the conversation; it gets noisy in here. It's so sad. I hope you get this guy."

"One more question Ginny. Did you happen to get a look at his car?"

"No, they sat in the booth I pointed to as we walked out. And the tables I work don't have a view of the parking lot."

Chapter 26

"Robbery/Homicide, Sergeant Miller."

"Yeah, I live in Trabuco Canyon, and I've got these neighbors, three guys, and they look like they're in their late twenty's, early thirty's. Well, actually one looks like he's in his early twenty's, but he's kind of strange and he's got a tattoo like the picture that was on the news. Anyway, most of the time he rides a Harley, but they have this old Ford Econoline van in their driveway. I thought it wasn't working, but the younger guy had it out this weekend with surfboards on it."

"What color's the van, sir?"

"It's white, but it's pretty dirty, and like I said, he had surfboards on it attached by a set of surf racks. And, with the tattoo on his arm with Harley Davidson wings, I thought I'd better call you guys."

"Do you know if there's any writing with the tattoo?"

"I don't know. I haven't gotten that close to him. The guy gives me the creeps."

It was one of several leads reported to the Investigative Hot-Line, but this one scored the highest thus far on the checklist. Hunter and Miller's Crown Vic left the back gate to the fleet parking lot, followed by Blackburn, Winslow, and Janowitz, in a marked patrol unit, all heading south toward Trabuco Canyon.

Located in the foothills of Orange County, Trabuco Canyon was named after a blunderbuss (firearm) lost during the expedition of Spanish explorer Gaspar de Portola. It is an eclectic mixture of custom estates, tract homes, and rural shacks off the grid. Hunter's team's destination would be a tract home that had seen better days. Located at the end of a cul de sac, the two story structure's shake roof was held in place by sap from the adjacent maple tree, probably also dating back to the Spanish explorers. The Ford van was backed up against the third car garage door, which appeared to have sustained a few bumper strikes over the years.

Miller requested two sheriff's units to assist, assigning them to the park located behind the suspect residence. Hunter and Miller would work their way down one side of the street, and Blackburn, Winslow, and Janowitz would approach on the opposite side, until both teams would reach the front door at the end of the cul de sac. Upon arrival at the park, they met the two assigned deputies, and discovered that one was a K-9 unit. They all switched to Orange South radio frequency to coordinate, then deployed.

Hunter and Miller drove to the corner house at the end of the suspect's street. Through binoculars, Hunter focused on the suspect's front door and determined that the hinge was on the left side. He radioed that he and Miller would take the door knob side, and would approach from the right side of the street. Blackburn, Winslow, and Janowitz would approach from the left. Hunter saw several adjacent yards with toys including Big Wheels and scooters scattered across lawns, driveways, and porches, causing concern children might at any moment enter a potential field of fire.

The team moved smoothly, darting in and out of porches and driveways, using parked cars and trucks as cover. One woman leaving her open garage, picked up her toddler, and ran back into the garage, when she saw Miller's blue windbreaker with its bold, white POLICE letters pass by. An unexpected crescendo of barking dogs reverberated throughout the neighborhood, and seemed to accelerate the pace, hastening their approach.

Both Hunter's and Blackburn's teams arrived on the porch within seconds of each other, and Miller notified the sheriff's deputies that they were knocking, and announcing in accordance with procedure. Suddenly, a sheriff's unit broadcasted over the radio:

"Unit 18 – K-2 (Canine)

"Unit 18 – K-2, Unit 39 –Lincoln 9 (Lt. Hunter)

"Unit 18 – K-2, subject matching 217 suspect (attempt murder) jumping backyard fence into park, heading northbound. K-9 deployed.

"Unit 39-Lincoln 9, copy. Making entry into res. (residence), checking for additional suspects.

"Unit 18 – K-2, Control 1 (County Dispatch Center)

"Control 1, Unit 18 – K-2?"

"Unit 18 – K-2, contact Station 91 (Orange County Fire Authority), request medics to intersection of Silvertree Ln. & Heritage Dr. We have 217 suspect in-custody at Trabuco Highland Central Park with K-9 bite to leg and arm. We'll transport him to meet medics at that 10-20 (location)."

"Unit 18 – K-2, Control 1, Station 91 is enroute."

Hunter's team checked the residence for any additional persons, and found the house empty. Hunter left Blackburn and Winslow on the porch to stand by, while he and Miller responded to the intersection to examine the suspect for tattoos and determine if he matched the attempted murder suspect's description. If he was "Trevor," they would need to apply for search warrants on both the house and the van.

Winslow shut the front door while they waited on the porch for Hunter's update. The smell inside the residence was incredibly overpowering, probably from accumulated spoiled food and trash. Winslow, known as a bit of a "neat-nick," felt it had been left long enough in that condition to deem it unfit. But it was Blackburn who paced and complained quite vocally, that he did not look forward to collecting and inventorying any evidence exposed to that much "olfactory contamination."

The residence was a flop house rental, which was certain to be a major annoyance of the unfortunate neighbors. It appeared to have three occupants, including the suspect, judging by the sleeping bags and air mattresses in each of the three bedrooms. While clearing through the residence searching for additional threats, there was little time to make note of any items that may have been in the van, which Amy might remember during a post-surgery interview. Judging by the condition of the house, it would be a safe guess that the van would be in similar condition.

Hunter radioed to the team that the forearm tattoo's inscription read, "Bury Me with My Harley." They had their suspect. But their hopes for linking this crime to the body dumps, was short lived. "Trevor," later discovered to be Tyler Moreland, was far from resembling an athletic, muscular man with a military style haircut. However, following the service of two search warrants in Trabuco Canyon, the discovery of Amy Van der Linden's DNA in the van, and Moreland's DNA on Amy, Atascadero State Prison would be "Trevor's" home for many years.

Chapter 27

The sky was overcast, and the temperature this Wednesday was in the high 60's, giving Steinhoffer perfect conditions to stage a video production of his test for pursuit terminating spike strips. The site of his experiment would be the parking lot for Veterans Memorial Stadium in Long Beach. Located near the campus of Long Beach City College, the stadium was home turf for all of Long Beach high schools and City College football games, and the parking lot served as venue for several swap meets and collectors' events. Today was a normal business day, with students going to classes, and arrivals and departures from the nearby airport in full operation, so the testing would hopefully not draw attention, nor be interrupted by on-lookers.

On site were four older model Ford Crown Victoria police cruisers stripped of all police equipment in preparation for change over to new units. Two marked police units, six sets of spare tires, and three sets of spike strips were staged for the test. Two mechanics from the police motor pool would drive the vehicles being pursued, and two additional mechanics were on scene to change tires. Two uniformed officers were assigned to drive the marked units, and two uniformed officers would be deploying the strips in front of the pursued vehicles. All personnel participating were working on their normal work day, so no overtime was being expended since they were performing the test while being paid their salaries as employees of the City of Long Beach.

Unlike the spikes found at garage entrances, pursuit terminating spikes are the approximate size of needles used with bicycle pumps to inflate basketballs and footballs. The tips are shaped like hypodermic needles – sharp and hollow, but thicker. Tires passing over them are punctured and rapidly deflate.

In addition to Chief Steinhoffer, members of the command staff included one deputy chief, one commander, and one lieutenant. The training sergeant and one officer assigned to the Training Bureau were present, and would be taking raw video footage of the trials for internal documentation. The video crew was provided by the vendor, Ruben Cohen of R.C. Enterprises, who was also in attendance. Noticeably absent, was Suzanne Duncan, Long Beach City Manager, who had not been notified of the event.

The first recorded test involved the two uniformed officers removing the spikes from the trunks of the patrol cars, removing their covers, and then pushing the strip of spikes across a spray painted lane of traffic. They would then pull a lever on the handle, raising the spikes from a horizontal position, to vertical, in preparation for a pursued vehicle. Both wide angle and close up shots were taken of each step in the procedure.

The second test demonstrated a mock pursuit, in which the strips were already in place, and the pursued vehicle passed over the vertical spikes. The tires began to deflate, and the officer quickly pulled back on the lever to retract the spikes, so that the police vehicle pursuing the suspect's car could pass over the strips without tire damage.

The final test depicted the entire process, with one officer opening the trunk to his cruiser, donning protective gloves, removing the strips from the trunk, placing them into the lane of traffic, and pulling the lever to deploy the spikes. The suspect's vehicle passes over the strip, the officer retracts the spikes to the horizontal position, and the police cruiser passes over. The last shot shows the suspect's vehicle with four deflated tires, and the "suspect" exiting and surrendering to the officers.

The total time for the set-up, staging, and take-down of the test was approximately three hours. Steinhoffer's only requirement for the vendor and the video crew was that the final production of the video have all Long Beach Police logos removed, or blotted out from patrol cars and uniform patches to eliminate any appearance of official or personal interest in the product by the Long Beach Police Department.

In theory, the plan was well organized, but, unfortunately for him, Steinhoffer had no way of knowing that R.C. Enterprises had either a disgruntled employee or mole, who had notified a competitor of the test, and that individual just happened to be standing near the corner of Conant St. and Faculty Avenue, taking his own video of the entire production.

Chapter 28

Swear-in day for Vannover was more of a celebratory event at Long Beach PD, than had been his experience with the Sheriff's Department. His mother and Aunt Erin were in attendance to witness his uncle, Chief Steinhoffer, swear him in, along with five other new officers who had just graduated from the Long Beach Police Academy.

He would first be assigned to the downtown area with his field training officer (FTO), Jerry Parker, a veteran of seven years. Parker had put on a few pounds since his academy days, but could write a pretty decent crime report, and was adept at recognizing ex-cons.

It didn't take long for Vannover to become familiar with the grid patterned streets in the downtown district. There were the usual bars that generated more than their share of assaults, but nothing compared to the history of "The Jungle," next to the former Pike amusement park.

In its heyday back in the 1940's and 50's, The Jungle had housed prostitutes, convicts, thieves, and down n' outers who preyed upon the Pike's clientele of sailors, teenagers, and tourists seeking thrill rides and carnival games. Around 1950, the city's redevelopment agency eliminated The Jungle and replaced it with the "Nu-Pike." Eventually that also disappeared, and in 1998 replaced it with the Aquarium of the Pacific, a host of restaurants, and a new convention center. But, even so, downtown districts do tend to attract crime, and continue to serve as great learning environments for new officers.

~

Chief Steinhoffer felt the time was now right to contact the entire roster of the exclusive club known as Cal Chiefs. The video was now edited down to one minute, and a website specifically created under the name of R.C. Enterprises / spike strips, was ready to showcase the devices. The message would go out on Chief Steinhoffer's letterhead encouraging his fellow chiefs to consider purchase of the pursuit terminating spike strips that his organization had just tested.

He would tell the chief that after having observed the company's presentation of the new technology for this equipment, he was so impressed that he had his department test them, and ordered sufficient numbers to equip one quarter of his marked patrol fleet. He would also say that thus far, he'd had five successful deployments in a month with no reported injuries to his officers. The letter would close with a referral to the website for video examples of the spike strips' unique features. He would include his non-published office phone number for any fellow member of Cal Chiefs for contact, should they have any questions.

~

Lena Holmquist had put up with enough badgering by the drunken truck driver, and the bartender was getting nervous that the encounter between the two patrons was reaching the point of physical violence. Lena had been quite the attraction in her day; but clearly alcohol had taken its toll in aging this Swedish bombshell. At 5'10" she had retained some of her classic curves, but the progressive leathering of her skin had become a roadmap of successive disappointments attributed to insecurities and addictions. Her once feathered blonde hair was now dishwater and matted. Yet even now her mere presence in this dive known as Long Beach's 322 Café, brought unwelcomed harassment.

Bartender Guiseppi Scotto had pleaded with her earlier to go home to her family, as he had done so many times before, when the former star of intimate wear commercials had become

116

disruptive. Now, her only semblance of class was the Cosmopolitan he had served her, in her effort to capture that spark of dignity given to girls who order drinks named in five syllables.

But, having once again failed to move her off the barstool, Scotto discreetly drew his cellphone from a back pocket, dialed 911, and spoke conversationally, allowing the police dispatcher to gather that she needed to send a unit quickly to fend off a brewing bar fight.

Vannover and Parker were two blocks away, finishing an F.I. card (field interview) on a homeless jaywalker, and sending him to a coffee shop with a $5.00 bill from Parker's wallet.

Arriving at the bar, Vannover and Parker watched the back side of a 60 year old, bearded biker with a swollen belly as he grabbed the stitching on Lena's blouse and she threw the remaining contents in her Cosmo glass toward his face. Vannover threw his right forearm around the biker's neck, and having secured the carotid restraint with his left hand, he dropped the biker to the floor, applying pressure. Within seconds the biker fell unconscious, was rolled onto his stomach, and Parker secured his hands with his pair of handcuffs.

While Vannover conducted his weapons search, Parker interviewed a shaking Lena, who, was now partially sobered by the groping.

"Ma'am, are you all right? From our vantage point, it appeared that this guy grabbed your breast. Is that correct?"

"Yes, and I want to press charges. He assaulted me."

"No problem. We'll need to fill out some paperwork here, after we put him in the back of our patrol car. This may require you to appear in court to testify if he doesn't plead guilty."

"I don't care; he assaulted me."

"Ma'am, it appears that you've had quite a bit to drink. How far away do you live?"

"Oh, a couple of miles."

"Can we call you a cab? Do you have enough money to pay for cab fare home?"

"Well, I'd planned on having a few more Cosmos before going home."

"I don't think that would be a wise choice. We can stay here, and make certain that you're safe in a cab before we leave."

"Ok, I get it. I'll leave; it wasn't my fault. But I'll go."

"You're probably right; it wasn't your fault. But I think Mr. Scotto's worried about your safety, as are we. I'll have our Dispatch send you a cab."

With Lena Holmquist safely tucked away in her cab, team Parker and Vannover headed to the station to book their suspect for sexual battery. Parker was impressed with the manner in which his trainee dispatched the biker, but wondered if he was wearing tighter uniform shirts, or if he was simply hitting the weight room more religiously. He should have suspected, but chose to ignore the possibility that this partner was actually cycling steroids.

Chapter 29

The first order of the R.C. Enterprises spike strips by an agency of substantial size was made by the Orange County Sheriff's Department that purchased ten sets of strips. The devices were placed in units assigned to their contract cities for testing before any larger numbers of procurement, as had been done with their current stock of Scorpion Spike Strips. Deputies went through roll call briefing training on policy and proper placement, with the requirement that written evaluations be completed following each deployment.

The Sheriff's Department had experienced success with the Scorpion Spike Strips in multiple pursuit terminating incidents, including a reserve fire engine stolen by a nineteen year old drunk driver. They had reported some small puncture wounds by deputies forgetting to don leather gloves. The department had been tracking results from other agencies. There was also, concern about the number of officers' injuries and deaths that were occurring across the nation resulting from improper deployment.

In addition, Orange County deputies were discovering that multiple pushing and pulling of the levers that raised and lowered the spikes during the training process were causing the rigidity in the cables to weaken. And, complaints communicated to the manufacturer were not being promptly addressed. CEO Ruben Cohen had been in Israel attempting to introduce a new rifle capable of firing around corners without exposing the shooter. His absence was becoming problematic, as his engineers were encountering difficulty in finding replacement materials that would not incur significant cost overruns.

~

It was Irvine's budget director, Kelly Stefano's birthday, and Suzanne Duncan was invited to a small gathering at Fornaio's Italian restaurant. Also invited were Irvine's Deputy Chief of Police, Jim Strauss, and Orange County Fire Authority Division Chief, Mason Koenig who were all friends that had worked together in Irvine.

Following their tiramisu dessert, Strauss, who had a reputation as a prankster, offered to share two videos on his cellphone along with a letter he brought that had been sent to all Cal Chief's members. He turned to Duncan and said, "Sounds like your chief is in the spike strip business."

Duncan's face immediately flushed red. She turned to Strauss and after seeming to have to compose herself, she finally said, "Well, this should be very interesting. I was not aware that Daniel had embarked on an entrepreneurial endeavor." All eyes turned to Duncan with alarm. Duncan was well known for her powerful speaking ability. And her, non-verbal display of awkwardness resulting from Strauss' announcement, took everyone by surprise.

Strauss began by reading portions of the letter, and played the "official" video that had obviously been professionally prepared. Then he ran a bootlegged version, that clearly displayed all the un-redacted Long Beach Police markings on patrol cars, and uniform shoulder patches.

A hush descended on the group, as Strauss announced that the bootlegged video was already running on the Internet. At this point only Kelly Stefano was aware of Duncan's relationship with Steinhoffer.

"But that's not all," added Strauss, sensing he now really had the group's attention. "I'm even hearing that O.C. Sheriffs are having trouble with the strips. Hope Steinhoffer only bought a few. And good thing he didn't do an on-camera endorsement. He'd really be catching some heat."

"I'm finding L.A. County law enforcement far less uptight about product endorsements. You'll frequently see LAPD and LASD (Sheriff) personnel in uniforms as models in equipment catalogues. Are we ready to settle the check? I've got a staff meeting in 45 minutes," Duncan responded. She was now in full damage control mode.

Chapter 30

The Tuesday afternoon traffic to Los Angeles was already loading up at 2:00 PM, and Dr. Erin O'Connell had hoped to arrive at the Holiday Inn near Westwood before rush hour turned the 405 freeway into gridlock. She had finished her last surgery for the day, a spinal fusion, and tomorrow morning she was scheduled to lecture at UCLA Medical Center. Rather than having to brave morning traffic on her day off, she reserved a hotel room near the campus, so she would be fresh for her presentation at 8:30 AM.

Wednesday morning's topic would address the Coflex implant, a titanium device surgically inserted between vertebrae to relieve the pressure of spinal stenosis by creating separation. The Food and Drug Administration had recently approved the instrumentation, and O'Connell had been one of several surgeons across the nation selected to test it on qualifying patients.

~

Chief Steinhoffer's text to Suzanne Duncan read as follows:

"Erin's in Westwood for the night. Lecture tomorrow - UCLA Med. Your house after Council mtg?"

Duncan's response:

"I've got champagne. Victoria's Secret awaiting..."

~

The 10:50 PM ending to the Long Beach City Council meeting roughly corresponded to the end of the Police Department's swing shift, and Vannover was in a hurry to play back the recording he had set on his TV of this evening's Anaheim Ducks hockey game. Chief Steinhoffer was also anxious to return home from the City Council meeting, after having received Duncan's romantic text. However, "home" tonight meant Newport Beach, where Suzanne's condominium was located.

Vannover's pickup truck cleared the secure lot, and soon entered the Port of Long Beach end of the 710 Freeway, heading for the 405 to Costa Mesa. Around the Brookhurst off ramp in Fountain Valley Vannover was passed by a green Ford Crown Victoria, traveling between 75-80 miles per hour in the fast lane. He immediately discarded his first thought that the "Crown Vic" probably belonged to his uncle, the Chief, who was traveling home to Shady Canyon. But then, he remembered the MacArthur Boulevard route his uncle had curiously taken after the JHAT exercise, and Vannover let that thought percolate as the Costa Mesa off ramp rapidly approached.

It was decided; the Ducks game could wait, his curiosity was calling. He would keep a loose tail on his uncle and find out what this mysterious destination could be. He signaled, and began taking the MacArthur off ramp by the airport, heading south toward Newport Beach.

Vannover had his suspicions; he had them since that breakfast at IHOP. He did some checking, and wrote down the address of the person he suspected, and then placed the paper in his glovebox. At the first red light, he pulled it out, and quickly entered it into his GPS in the event that he lost the tail.

He kept behind the Crown Vic as it made a partial turn onto Jamboree Road, the northernmost point of the Back Bay. The full moon overhead reflected brightly onto the water, and with the increased illumination he could see that he was passing some astronomically expensive neighborhoods. His head swiveled left to right, recognizing Fashion Island, Balboa Island, and then suddenly he had to make a quick left, onto Back Bay Drive. Tension began to rise in Vannover's gut, fearing that he would be noticed since there were diminishing numbers of cars on this road.

He saw Steinhoffer turn onto Villa Point Drive off a traffic circle at the end of Back Bay Drive, but Vannover kept following the circle around, heading in the opposite direction. He knew that if he'd continued following the car, his uncle would know he was being tailed. So he pulled to the right and parked.

Vannover expanded his GPS to get a broader picture of the neighborhood, and discovered that Villa Point Drive became a private road with a gate which he could probably not access. He was so focused on avoiding detection he'd temporarily forgotten that the person, with whom he suspected his uncle was cheating, actually lived in a condo on Villa Point Drive, overlooking Pacific Coast Highway. Displayed on the paper lying on his passenger seat was the name and address for Long Beach City Manager, Suzanne Duncan.

~

Steinhoffer's heart raced as his hands fumbled a set of keys to Duncan's condo out of his pocket. He found his own key to her front door opened it, and called out, "Sweetheart, I'm home!"

Suzanne Duncan came out of the kitchen into the entry holding two fluted champagne glasses filled with a bubbling portion of Korbel, and handed one to Steinhoffer. He held his breath momentarily, gazing with lips parted, at Duncan's pink nightgown. Two spaghetti straps held the satin gown in place, as it cascaded over her ample breasts to her ankles.

As he moved towards her to embrace, she extended her left index finger into the sternum of his chest, stopping his advance, as she held the champagne flute in her right hand next to her cheek. Duncan's lips pursed and her eyebrows narrowed as she began to speak.

"You neglected to inform me that you had proceeded with your little investment plan for terminating pursuits."

"Well I ..."

"Stop! Did you give your "friend" Reuben any money?"

"Just some seed money, only $15,000."

"Did I not warn you?"

"Who told you?"

"That's not important. What is important is the fact that <u>you</u> didn't tell <u>me</u>."

"Did you know that there's a YouTube video running on the Internet showing City of Long Beach patrol car markings, and clearly identifiable Long Beach PD shoulder patches, on City personnel testing those spike strips? If that wasn't an endorsement, then you removed any doubt by sending that message on letterhead to Cal Chiefs."

"Look Suzanne, from our last discussion on this topic, you made it pretty clear that you were reluctant to become involved in the opportunity, so I went ahead on my own."

"Yes, you certainly did. But you failed to comprehend that my reservations applied to both of us, and you didn't have the courtesy, or the foresight to give me, as your boss, the head's up that this thing was going down. Have you even heard that there have been problems with the reliability of this product?"

"Yes, and we've been working on developing a solution..."

"Let's get this straight. There should be no "we" in this. You need to make this whole thing right, and then divest yourself of any association with this product and company. Get Reuben to replace the faulty parts on these spike strips immediately, even if it bankrupts the company. He's got other products to keep himself in business, but you've staked the City's reputation and your own on this boondoggle."

"I'm sorry; I'll get on it first thing tomorrow..."

"And by the way, I want you to think about this. (Gesturing with her free hand swinging from her face down her flowing nightgown.) This is what you could have had tonight, but you screwed it up. You may leave now."

126

Chapter 31

The weekend had finally arrived, and it was not only Vannover's day off, but he had been released from his training officer, and would now be allowed to ride alone or with a partner. The advantage of being assigned to a field training officer (FTO) was having weekend days off since FTO's had seniority, and generally worked weekdays. The disadvantage was that, next week, he would be working nights with Wednesdays, Thursdays, and Fridays off, a shift of which he was quite familiar after having worked for the Sheriff's Department.

His plan was to drop off his pickup truck at the mechanic's shop, rent a car for the day, and go to the range to shoot his off-duty pistols. He had made lunch plans with a waitress he met at the IHOP across from the airport, and would meet her at Islands restaurant following his target practice.

When it came to firearms, Vannover was very methodical in his habits, down to the very clothes that he put on in preparation for this ritual. A particular long sleeve white t-shirt was required, with the distinctive markings of the Baker to Vegas Challenge Cup Relay, an annual all-night desert race involving over 200 teams of law enforcement officers. Next, he wore a pair of khaki 5.11 tactical pants, with multiple pockets capable of holding equipment ranging from ammunition magazines, Leatherman all-purpose tools, to cell phones. Finally, one pair of black, polished Blackhawk SWAT boots with Vibram soles, completed his uniform of the day.

Vannover dropped off his truck, and unloaded his range bag into the parts delivery truck for his mechanic's repair shop. The owner's son would drop him off at the airport car rental level, where he would select his preferred statement of ruggedness with class: the British Range Rover.

He rented a white Rover, and headed southbound on the 405 toward Mission Viejo. His destination was On Target, an indoor range located in a long strip of industrial businesses adjacent to an Amtrak depot. The California Highway Patrol frequently occupied the law enforcement section, and the remainder was open to the public.

An interesting assortment of shooters frequented the range. There were usually only a handful of excellent marksmen and women present. But there was always the guy who had the pistol with all the accoutrements, most of which he didn't need. Once you glanced at his target, you would have thought he was shooting birdshot out of a 12- gauge shotgun. Ten-ring bullseyes were accidents. The scariest shooters were those who brought their girlfriends who had never shot. These young ladies, dressed in tight blue jeans and pastel collared blouses, would become frustrated in their marksmanship, or lack thereof, and would turn away from their targets to complain, losing track of their pistol barrels, while shooters to the right and the left dropped to the ground.

Vannover arrived at his target bay, and placed his range bag on the bench behind. He retrieved two pistols, a Glock 26, 9mm, and a Beretta Jet-fire .25 caliber, and set them on the counter that separated two walls that constituted the bay. A box of 9mm rounds was opened, and then loaded into the Glock. The silhouette target was then clipped to the cross beam attached to the automatic cable for target placement. Vannover chose a distance of 15 yards, and began a series of single shots, placing most in the center mass 8 & 10 rings.

After switching in a fresh target, he sent it down range, and loaded the Beretta .25 caliber. Although the Glock he had just fired was considered a concealable pistol, the Beretta was significantly smaller, and a grip adjustment was required to avoid contact with the slide that would be ejecting spent shells.

Unfortunately, Vannover became distracted by the hot blonde, two bays over, and failed to check his grip before engaging the target and firing. A mili-second after pulling the trigger, the slide ejected the shell, and in doing so, traversed below the first joint in his thumb, slicing the skin open. He continued firing a couple more rounds before realizing from the pain, that he had opened up a deep wound; and blood had spilled onto the counter, over the bullets seated in their plastic holders protruding from open boxes, and onto the floor covered with shell casings for various caliber rounds.

Vannover grabbed the first aid kit from his range bag, and wound a Koban adhesive wrap around his thumb to stop the blood flow. He held the wrap in place, and carefully unloaded the Beretta, and packed up all his gear. After returning to the Range Rover, he slowly unwrapped the Koban, and saw that the bleeding had stopped. After a few careful swipes with a sterile wipe, he placed two butterfly strips in the shape of an "X" across the wound, and he was ready to go. Frustrated by the injury, and the abridged target practice, Vannover's growling stomach reminded him of the lunch date awaiting him at Islands.

As he approached the Crown Valley Parkway exit on the northbound 405 Freeway, Vannover discovered that his butterfly strips had soaked through, indicating that his wound would need suturing. He phoned his lunch date to reschedule, then drove to the outpatient clinic near Islands to have his laceration closed.

~

The 3:00 PM Irvine Police Department swing shift briefing began, as usual, with the patrol sergeant reading the "boards" to the "troops." It was appropriate that it was Sergeant Richard Austin's turn to have the honors. Five minutes into his summary of the crimes occurring during the previous 24 hours, he was interrupted by visitors who had entered the rear of the briefing room. Standing by the back row of chairs stood Lt. Scott Hunter, Detective Tom Blackburn, and Detective Stephanie Winslow who was holding Amy Van der Linden's hand.

Following several cranial and facial surgeries, Amy felt that she had recovered sufficiently to thank the officers who had come to her aid the day she was assaulted in the rock quarry. Hunter introduced her to the shift, taking special care to avoid any mention of the sexual crime, by simply stating, "Amy was the victim in our 217 (Attempted Murder)."

Austin rose from his chair at the front table facing the officers, and began to walk toward the back of the room, but was met halfway by Amy, who ran to embrace the crusty, but tearful senior sergeant. The officers in the room rose to their feet, as the walls reverberated from the thunderous applause. It was a motivational moment for Irvine PD's Delta Shift.

~

Two stitches, and Vannover's laceration was closed. One tetanus shot, with a course of antibiotics, and he was on his way. The Range Rover had some dried blood on the steering wheel, which was brought to the attention of the rental car attendant, before Vannover departed for the curb to await the arrival of his ride from the auto repair shop. Neither he, nor the attendant knew, however, that there was more than blood remaining in the Rover.

Chapter 32

Kari Patterson's flight was on time, and her excitement grew as the wheels of her plane struck the runway abruptly, signaling that she was home. The Baylor University senior would soon see her parents, along with many of her Tesoro High School friends who would be attending Amanda Mellenger's wedding. Her parents would have preferred to have picked her up, as was the normal procedure for John Wayne Airport arrivals, but this weekend Kari wanted to make a statement to her friends that she was on her way to success. Her internship with a Manhattan public relations firm taught her the importance that image played in selling a product, and now within striking distance of her bachelor's degree, she would package that image with proper transportation.

The car rental agency had one Range Rover available, a white one. Although the controls and instrument panel were somewhat confusing in comparison to her Subaru, she felt she could figure it out sufficiently to get her home to Mission Viejo.

Kari's left turn onto MacArthur Boulevard went well, but she needed to merge to the right one more lane in order to catch the on-ramp to the southbound 405 Freeway. It was then that she realized that she had not properly adjusted her mirrors. She moved into the far right lane failing to notice the Ford F150 pickup traveling at approximately 50 miles per hour, with the driver texting his girlfriend.

The impact into the Range Rover's trunk area was hard, but fortunately the gas tank did not ignite. However, Kari's neck snapped forward and back in the classic whiplash motion, but avoiding a cervical break by striking the headrest. She sat, stunned, with a small trickle of blood visible from her nose. The

F150's airbag deployed, pinning the driver in his seat. Several motorists in adjacent lanes dialed 911 on their cell phones, and two witnesses stayed at the scene checking on the welfare of both drivers.

Around the block an Engine Company from Orange County Fire Authority (OCFA) Station 28 exited onto Gillette Avenue, heading toward the crash. In addition, Irvine PD motorcycle Unit 39-512 arrived moments later, while Civilian Traffic Accident Investigator Unit 39-524 was dispatched to take the report. Traffic began to back up to Campus Drive, slowing the arrival of a Medix ambulance which was traveling from neighboring Newport Beach.

After placing a cervical collar around Kari's neck, OCFA paramedics carefully lifted her onto a gurney which was then taken by Medix attendants and loaded into the ambulance. Paramedic John Hernandez joined Kari for the ride to Western Medical Center in Tustin where she would be evaluated. Aside from some minor chemical burns from the airbag, the driver of the pickup was not injured.

Prior to Kari's departure, Civilian Traffic Accident Investigator (CTI) Mary Cowdrey, had obtained driver's licenses and registration from both drivers, and taken custody of Kari's purse, suitcase, and laptop, placing them into her van for later booking into safekeeping at the station. She'd then called tow trucks for both vehicles, marked the pavement around the tires with spray paint to record their positions, and then quickly begun to fill out the California Highway Patrol (CHP) 180 form on the Range Rover. The CHP 180 authorized storage of the inoperable vehicle, and inventoried its contents for the owner.

As a former student and cheerleader at Santa Margarita Catholic High School, CTI Cowdrey was the consummate traffic investigator. In her powder blue uniform shirt, navy blue pants, and spit polished shoes, she was the image of efficiency and

132

competence. The printing on her accident reports was immaculate, and the detail was so comprehensive that the Traffic Bureau routinely included her on call-outs to major collisions and traffic fatalities.

After including Kari's luggage and personal effects on the inventory, Cowdrey re-entered the Rover to check for any additional items left inside the vehicle. Under the front passenger seat on the floorboard she located a woman's hairbrush, which she first assumed were thrown from Kari's purse upon impact. However, to her surprise, under to driver's seat she found two - empty shell casings from a small caliber pistol.

She gathered the items, placed them into a clear, plastic zip lock baggie, and recorded them on the 180 inventory: "two (2) small caliber shell casings, (poss. .22)." She would follow up at the hospital with Kari for her statement, and try to determine if she had any knowledge regarding the origin of the ammunition.

~

Kari's parents arrived at Western Medical Center where she was released to them, wearing her neck brace, having suffered a minor whiplash. They then went to the Irvine Police station where CTI Cowdrey was finishing up dictating the narrative to her accident report. The property and evidence technician brought Kari her purse, laptop, suitcase, and the small baggie containing the shell casings.

When Kari said she was positive the shell casings did not belong in her property, the technician made a notation on the inventory form for the Rover's legal owner, Paragon Executive Coaches. He then advised Kari that the casings would be returned to the legal owner, and wished her a speedy recovery from her injuries.

Chapter 33

Hunter began his morning reading the 24-hour log at his desk, eating an apple cinnamon muffin while sipping his cup of Kona. He had requested that any reports, crimes or incidents involving Range Rovers have a notation on the daily log. Seeing that a Range Rover had been involved in an injury traffic collision at MacArthur and the 405, he walked downstairs to the Records Bureau to retrieve the report.

The Records clerk advised him that the report had not been received by them, but was listed in the system as "Waiting for Narrative." He then walked over to the watch commander's desk, and located the face page and CHP 180 form that was in the "Hold" bin. On the face page he noted that the driver of the Range Rover was a 20 year old female from Mission Viejo. Turning the page, he found the CHP 180, and saw that among the property booked for safekeeping was a baggie containing two small caliber shell casings (possibly .22).

Intrigued by this discovery, Hunter walked to the Property/Evidence room, and asked the technician to pull the baggie booked under the traffic accident case number. When he emptied them onto the counter and asked for a magnifying glass, he saw they were actually .25 calibers, and the primers were indented, indicating that they had been fired. He also discovered that each shell casing appeared to have blood stains on it. A margin note on the evidence slip read, "Ret. To Veh. L/O," (Return to vehicle legal owner).

Now even more intrigued at this turn of events, Hunter quickly phoned Blackburn, and asked him to bring down a Sheriff's Crime Lab request for analysis form. He then made a notation on the property form that the shell casings were seized as evidence, and called the storage yard to put an immediate hold on the Range Rover.

~

Hunter and Blackburn's drive to the airport was filled with anticipation. Now they had a Range Rover and .25 caliber shell casings with blood. Next they needed to find out who the previous drivers for that vehicle had been. So their next step was the car rental desks located at the lower level where airport arrivals were picked up, across from the larger than life size statue of John Wayne.

This landmark always reminded Hunter of his swear-in as an Irvine police officer in the office of the city's first police chief, who kept a framed sketch of the famous actor posted on the wall. He had been surprised by the informality of the "ceremony," that was a big contrast to his first, at the Los Angeles Police Academy when he was in his dress blues. However, he'd soon learned that the casualness of the event would belie the organizational culture of a department where "good" would not suffice, it had to be great. Command performances in court were the norm, and case preparation was expected to be so comprehensive that testimony was seldom required.

He knew that he would need to draw on all of his training, experience, and leaderships skills to put this homicidal puzzle together.

~

Paragon Executive Coaches was a specialty rental agency catering to drivers seeking exotic sports cars, elegant sedans, and the most exclusive sport utility vehicles. Hunter and Blackburn were met at the counter by Patti Nilsson, a striking 5'2" former San Diego State University cheerleader who was paid handsomely to showcase the image of the automobiles their agency featured.

Following introductions, Nilsson turned her computer screen showing both detectives the history on the white Range Rover, which was brief as it was the current year's model. Preceding Kari Patterson's rental were the names of only two men: first, Alex Vannover, and before him, Larry Giroux.

"Patti, would you happen to know this Alex Vannover? Does he rent frequently with your agency?" Blackburn asked, quickly scribbling the name on his notepad.

"Yes, he was a sheriff's deputy who worked here at John Wayne. He liked Range Rovers, and would occasionally rent with us."

"You said was. He's no longer with the Sheriff?"

"I heard he went to Long Beach. He said his uncle's the chief."

"What was he like?"

"He's a flirt, friendly, but a bit of a bragger. Is he in some kind of trouble?"

"No, there was just something left in the car."

"Oh? Did we forget to get everything cleaned out from the previous driver? I thought you guys were here investigating the accident. What did we miss? I'll have to talk to the housekeeping crew."

"Well, we can't go into that right now. It might be some evidence that got left behind."

"Do you have any knowledge about this Larry Giroux?

"Oh yes, he's another Sheriff's deputy who also occasionally comes in to rent one of our Rovers."

"Do you have any silver Rovers?"

"We had a couple, but they were sold and replaced with two white ones and a new silver one."

"Do you have records on who rented the silver Rovers?"

"Yes, they're archived. I'll have to get back with you on those records."

137

"If you would please, here's my card with my cell phone number."

Chapter 34

As Blackburn ran firearms registered to Vannover, Hunter stood by, thinking about the complications that could be involved in the possibility of criminality within the ranks. Then Hunter queried the search engine on his cell phone to check the Long Beach PD website. The Chief of Police was still Irvine's former chief, Steinhoffer, so, their last names were different. He'd have to check elsewhere to see if there was a familial connection. He started by asking Blackburn if he had any friends at Long Beach PD.

"Yeah, I've got a guy in Detectives," Blackburn replied as his screen showed the handguns registered to Vannover. They included a Glock 26, 9mm pistol, and a Beretta Jet-fire .25 caliber semi-automatic. Hunter began to mentally list the steps he needed to take next. He knew police organizations were often fraught with gossip. Reputations could be ruined, cases could be compromised. They would need to be discreet, and strive to keep the politics at bay by not alerting the Long Beach Police Department about all of this.

"Tom, have we gotten the bloodwork back on those .25 caliber shells yet?"

"No, it's on my list. I'll give them a call in about 20 minutes. They're usually at lunch right now."

"And what about CSI? Did they find any additional blood inside that white Rover at the storage yard?"

"Norbett's there right now, working it. Hey Scott, what are your thoughts on how the shell casings got there? Do you think she was shot there, and they just got the color wrong on the car? Or was there another homicide in the white Rover that we haven't yet discovered?"

"Man, it could be either of those scenarios, Tom, or he simply tracked the shells into the car after they got lodged between the treads of his shoes."

~

Suzanne Duncan took the last sip of her French roast, and nearly choked as she watched the news ticker running across the bottom of the screen of Good Morning America: "Kansas City police officer in critical condition after failed deployment of spike strips..." She had that sixth sense of doom, that the cause was mechanical, and that the manufacturer was that dreadful company in which Daniel had gotten himself and the City entangled. She turned to the mirror to make one last check before heading out the door to her Mercedes and off to work.

Chapter 35

At 2300 hours (11:00 PM) Hunter finished the last sentence on a report documenting his involvement in the early morning arrest of a robbery suspect. He enjoyed keeping connected to the operations in the field, but the paperwork diverted precious time needed in coordinating the homicides. He was one of those cops who frequently experienced crimes and their perpetrators falling in his lap, and accepted the additional work as a reward for maintaining situational awareness.

Hunter moved on to his in-basket and signed off on Norbett's CSI supplemental report indicating that he was unable to find any additional blood present in the white Range Rover. The next document requiring attention was from the County Crime Lab. There was, however enough blood on the shell casings to identify as type "A" positive. DNA results were still pending.

Remembering that he had not heard from Patti Nilsson from Paragon Executive Coaches regarding the rental record of the silver Rovers, he pulled a microcassette recorder that he occasionally used for interviews, from his coat pocket, placed it on his desk, and played back the interview hoping that she had provided him a contact number. Fortunately she had.

Hunter's attention was interrupted by the shadow of a figure blocking his open door, and the clearing of a throat. Lieutenant Michael O'Brien stood with his classic smirk and basketball belly pushing the buttons on his uniform shirt, worn for the third day in a row. Hunter quickly pushed the off button on the recorder.

"Burning the midnight oil again Hunter?"

Hunter glanced up, wondering when that guy would get some new clichés.

"Yes Michael, I'm assuming you read the daily log, and saw that we caught a residential robbery suspect this morning."

"I did Scott. Maybe if you would avoid these entanglements, you might solve a murder or two, and not have to stay late anymore. Or you could join me in Patrol and play gun fighter all you want."

"Thanks Michael, always appreciate your sage advice. Have you started any, excuse me, heard any good rumors today?"

"Bye-Bye Hunter. Happy Trails..."

Hunter returned to his in-basket, but stopped when a pretty blonde wearing a ponytail and tight workout clothes stood in his doorway. Dispatcher Valerie Mason had just finished her shift, and appeared to be heading to the gym on the city hall side of the civic center.

"Hi Scott, I hardly ever see you anymore."

"Valerie, what a surprise. Yeah, been working a lot of long hours lately."

"I can imagine. Are you close to finding a suspect in those body dumps?"

"We just need a little luck, and we'll have all the pieces to the puzzle."

"Good. How's Ashley? We sure miss her up in Dispatch."

"Oh she's fine. She's new at American Airlines, so she got the crummy shifts. But it's OK right now. Since I've been working these homicides I haven't been available. Hopefully we'll get this wrapped up, and we can take a vacation."

"Sounds great. Please say hello for me."

"Will do."

Valerie departed from the Bureau into the hallway leading to the gym. Quietly following after having been seated behind the partition near Hunter's office was Lt. Michael O'Brien gathering information. The bright red light on Hunter's microcassette, indicated that he had pushed the record button in error. He tapped the stop button, and continued collating clues.

~

As the midnight hour approached, Lt. O'Brien checked out a patrol cruiser. It was his habit to drive around in the field and follow up on calls for service before the radio traffic wound down. He was known to fall asleep behind the watch commander's desk at approximately 4:00 AM, and awaken before 6:00, as the Day Watch officers prepared for morning briefing. O'Brien was also known to use the Mobile Data Computer (MDC) in his patrol car to send personal messages, much like the private messaging system on Facebook. Frequently, those communiques transmitted rumors regarding personnel he distained.

The Chief was at the top of his list. Not that the current occupant of the ivory tower was an autocrat, but, rather that O'Brien felt he should be the chief. He viewed himself as a Wild West marshal, and Chief Roger Chesterton as a blue-suited bureaucrat.

Other members of O'Brien's list were those considered to be the fair-haired boys, who because of their clean appearance, education, and what he termed "counterfeit work ethic," were given unearned opportunities. He viewed Hunter as a classic example of this particular category of officer, and would try to undermine him or minimize his accomplishments whenever possible.

O'Brien saw Hunter's brief encounter with Valery Mason as a great opportunity to create mischief for the "fair haired" Lieutenant Hunter. As soon as he could get into his patrol car, O'Brien went to work. He intended this evening's MDC transmission to go to Officer Darrel Ayers. However, the meat of O'Brien's gossip ended up being transmitted to all terminals, when his "Reply All" key was depressed. Whether O'Brien really only intended this juicy tidbit to go to Ayres, or whether the

143

keystroke hit was accidental, would be open to speculation but the content was devastating:

"...reference my suspicions regarding the liaison between Hunter and Mason. I have it on good authority that it's a confirmed kill..."

Valery Mason's initial introduction to the O'Brien broadcast libel came as she walked past the Dispatch Center's window. Two dispatchers waved frantically toward her to enter the Center before she could head to the locker room for her shower. Initially, Valery was flattered that someone would link her to Hunter, but she soon realized that feelings couldn't help but be hurt, and reputations damaged. Her first call was to Ashley Horton, not thinking that a better choice would have been to Hunter, to give him an opportunity for a defense.

~

Fortunately for Hunter, Ashley was familiar with the dynamics and personalities within the department, having worked there for several years prior to her employment with American Airlines. She strongly encouraged Valery to file a complaint with Internal Affairs the following day. Hunter was understandably furious, and phoned Dispatch, directing that Lt. O'Brien call his cellphone immediately. The call was never returned.

Chapter 36

The annual Jimmy Buffett concert date had arrived, and the Irvine Meadows Amphitheater had now become Margaritaville. The parking lot was jammed with cars, trucks, and campers, transforming the entire venue into one big drunken party. Banks of port-a-potties were not enough to handle the enormous crowd of concertgoers filled with Tequila, beer, and narcotics and the lines for each outhouse were at least twenty deep.

Some high-end revelers went so far as to bring their own sand and palm trees, and place them on the asphalt next to their motorhomes. Teams of police and paramedics walked the expansive parking lot breaking up fights, and tending to injuries ranging from tumbles off campers, to hibachi burns.

Arrests were numerous, and primarily attributed to public intoxication. The most unique enforcement intervention resulted when two entrepreneurs posted a sign on their station wagon offering a free beer to women who would flash their breasts for them. Irvine officers shut down the operation on the grounds of prostitution, providing consideration (goods, services, or money) for a sex act.

In the midst of this carnival atmosphere and debauchery was Larry Giroux, the currently off-duty Sheriff's Special Deputy from the airport, who brought his newly acquired girlfriend, Amber Morgan, to their seats in the orchestra section of the amphitheater. Seated next to them was an unknown, middle aged couple, celebrating their 15th wedding anniversary. The husband was seated next to Amber, and asked her if she had ever gone to a Buffett concert before, and she answered that she had not. Larry, who had consumed too many margaritas to exercise rational judgement took issue with this perceived flirtation, and slapped Amber across her face.

Unfortunately for Amber, the slap caught the eyelid of her left eye, causing it to swell shut. Larry, suddenly a bit sobered, realized he needed to take Amber to the medics. As Amber was receiving treatment, Larry recognized that the paramedics would be calling the police, so he left for the parking lot immediately. Too drunk to drive, he stayed in the parked white Range Rover, and attempted to sleep it off. Following the dressing of her wounds, Amber told the officer that she was not interested in pressing charges, or probably any future as Larry's girlfriend, and called a girlfriend to come pick her up.

Leaving the victim with an option in the event that she changed her mind, the officer took an "incident," rather than crime report, and gave Amber the case number for future reference. Special Deputy Giroux's law enforcement career was suddenly balancing on a precipice.

Chapter 37

The friendly game of cards was becoming tedious to Lena Holmquist, so the wine flowed more generously. She and her husband Lars had invited the Petersons over for a Friday night game of hearts. They both enjoyed the company of their fellow immigrants who had sought a better future for their families. The Holmquist's three kids, Andrea, age 8, Ilsa, age 7, and Sven, age 3, were playing in the family room with the Peterson's twins, Ingrid and Isabella, age 6, while the adults played cards in the kitchen.

Lena was celebrating her good fortune of having avoided courtroom testimony, following the guilty plea to sexual battery by her biker assailant, Rusty Adderly. He was out on bail, pending his sentencing hearing in two weeks.

The snail paced game of hearts gave Lena anxiety, prompting her to put an old record on the turntable, and begin dancing solo around the kitchen table. With no takers willing to become her partner, she downed another glass of Cabernet, and announced that she was taking a walk. Lars and the Petersons looked on in dismay, but concluded that a walk in the cold night air might be the best antidote for her increasing inebriation.

As she drew closer to the bus stop near her Locust Avenue house, she watched the Long Beach Transit District bus that could take her downtown stopped at the red light. She considered returning home, but the prospect of continued boredom prompted her to jump on board hoping to attract more attention to her rapidly fading Scandinavian beauty.

The 322 Café was bustling with activity and loud music reverberated from the classic 50's juke box. Men of varying ages and two to three women of questionable sources of income hovered around the bar counter, while a handful of couples were seated at tables on a floor littered with scores of peanut shells. Located on East 1st Street, the café was a relic from the past, when Long Beach was a home port for the Navy, and the shipyards were actively keeping the fleet seaworthy.

Lena's entrance was discreet. Her desire to draw attention was tempered by her need to first survey the premises to determine if there was anyone worth showing an interest. A swarthy, sixty year old turned from his bar stool, giving her room at the counter, and offered her a drink. She politely declined, stating that she appreciated his courtesy, but established a rule that her first drink be purchased on her own. Her experience told her this tactic made her a challenge worth pursuing more often than not. The Cabernet had faded during her walk and the bus ride, so it seemed to her that it was time to order her favorite Cosmopolitan.

The Petersons had left over an hour ago, and the Holmquist kids had all been tucked into bed. Lars began to experience the familiar sense of concern his free-spirited, alcoholic wife was, as usual, venturing into trouble. However, there was no way he was going to initiate a search for her and leave the children unattended.

After her second refill, the high she was experiencing began to settle in. Now Lena felt as though the eyes of every man in the establishment were focused directly on her. The men in their 50's on either side of her barstool kept offering her drinks, but by this time she was struggling to even put a sentence together much less convincingly establish her boundaries. She knew she needed to leave, but wasn't sure if she had enough money left in her purse for cab fare, and couldn't remember the bus schedule for this time of night.

Exiting the café entrance, the cold air against her face gave Lena a moment of sobriety as she walked slowly toward the nearby bus stop. A cab driver on the opposite side of the street watched as a pickup truck stopped by the sheltered bench. The driver got out and approached her, and the cab driver could see they had a momentary conversation. She was last seen by him entering the passenger side of the truck and driving off.

Chapter 38

The early morning fog hovered over the oilfield located at the 3400 block of Locust Avenue near the intersection of Long Beach Boulevard and Wardlow. Police tape cordoned off a large swath of land covered with oil wells. Long Beach Police Detective Sergeant Jason Horne stood over the supine body of Lena Holmquist, lying at the edge of the field, where she had been found earlier by a newspaper delivery boy.

Her floral dress was hiked up above her waist. Her shoes had been tossed approximately ten feet from her body, and her panties were stuffed into her mouth. Semen still liquefied on her abdomen indicated evidence of sexual assault, and the cause of death appeared to be a gunshot wound to the head by a small caliber round.

The coroner's team had just arrived, and rotated Holmquist's body onto its side, revealing an exit wound on the back side of her head. The bullet's path tracked from a contact hit to the forehead with powder burns approximately an inch below the hairline, and out the back of the skull. Horne quickly called out to the coroner's assistant, "Hold her there for a second, please. Let me check the soil underneath where her head was."

Horne pulled his Tanto-bladed knife out from his belt, and carefully sifted through the dirt. The blade struck a hard object, which he lifted, and gently blew the dirt clear of. Resting on the blade of his knife was a .25 caliber slug with dried blood on the flat end that fit into the shell casing. Horne photographed it, as well as the soil from where it was retrieved. He then placed it in a tiny evidence envelope, and put it in his blazer pocket.

Horne's lead detective, Bob Luther, who had recently transferred from background investigations to Homicide, stood by taking copious notes, along with an occasional photo from his cell phone camera to assist in preparing his crime scene diagram. Since childhood this had been an assignment he had dreamed of achieving, so he really wanted to do everything right. The appearance of this scene, reminded him of a crime flyer he had recently received from Orange County that bore similarities. But because there were differences, he was reluctant to bring it up, or risk getting sidetracked.

However, he wanted to say something, so he said, "Hey Sarge, the obvious first suspect would be the guy who just pleaded guilty to assaulting her at the 322 Café, wouldn't he?

When Luther could see that he had Horne's attention, he continued.

"Well, last week we got an alert flyer from Irvine about some homicides they're working involving .25 auto's, with attractive female victims. They've got Range Rover SUV's as suspect vehicles; we obviously don't have a vehicle yet, but, if this crime fits the pattern of the ones on the flyer, I'm thinking we should at least look at the suspect in the other cases. "I heard our court liaison officer complaining yesterday she had to track down two of our officers, last minute to take them off call for court. The suspect wasn't expected to plead guilty. Judge let him out on bail until sentencing."

"Where's this suspect live?"

"He's a local. According to the flyer, he stays at the Travelodge downtown."

"Any other details before we send a team over there to pick him up?"

"Maybe we'll get one when this case hits the news. Let's have a chat with him before we lose some evidence. Do you know who's working the Irvine case?"

"Yeah, Tom Blackburn, he's a friend; I'll give him a call."

Chapter 39

It seemed to Hunter that a lot of time had passed since he and Ashley had spent any quality time with each other. She was in town this weekend, but Hunter needed to stay close to home as the serial homicide cases were coming together.

Still, he had been waiting a long time for the conversation with Ashley he had planned for the evening. And it was important for it to be held in just the right place.

Hunter drove to Sand Canyon Drive past the Irvine Country Store. Taking a dirt road up the hill and through the orchards, Hunter pointed out to Ashley a foreman's bungalow, which he had wanted for some time to show her. The green painted clapboard construction had a quaint porch and hardware from another generation that made it feel like a scene from Knott's Berry Farm. He went to her side of the car, opened the door for her and as soon as she was standing next to him he began a narrative he had rehearsed for several months.

"The Irvine Ranch has this on the list for demolition for development, so our SWAT team was allowed access to practice entries and launch tear gas before they tore it down. When I was on the team, we spent a day up here running several training evolutions before I realized the view. It was a clear day like this, and you can see all the way to Newport Beach. See? That's Fashion Island, near the beach. Now, look beyond the shore, and below those clouds."

"Oh my lord, you can see Catalina Island!"

"Yes you can sweetheart. It's 26 miles out to sea, and you are viewing it right now."

"It's spectacular!"

"Yep, and I have a friend who's a planner with the Irvine Company, and they have planned to build a community up here, as part of the build-out of the City of Irvine. I want to live here. Actually, I want to live here with you Ashley."

Hunter then dropped to one knee, and retrieved from his pocket a small jewelry box. He opened it revealing the diamond engagement ring inside and began to speak from his heart.

"Ashley Horton, I have loved you from the moment I first saw you at the police station. I knew that someday this moment would arrive, and that I would be as nervous as I am now. But I promise you this; if you say "yes," to becoming my bride, I will love you as long as I live, and cherish every moment that we can share together. What do you say, Sweetheart? Will you marry me?"

"Yes! Of course it's yes. You're so crazy. When did you think this up?"

"It's been a couple months trying to figure out how to do this."

As he slipped the ring on her finger and rose to his feet, they embraced and kissed as the afternoon breeze blew her auburn hair, caressing her shoulders.

"What's inside the cooler in the backseat, Lieutenant Hunter?"

"It's a small bottle of champagne, and a red rose, with baby's breath, for celebrating, soon to be Mrs. Lieutenant Hunter..."

Chapter 40

"Detective Blackburn?"

"Yes."

"This is Patti Nilsson with Paragon Executive Coaches."

"Yes Patti, I remember you."

"Lieutenant Hunter had asked me to check our archives on those two silver Range Rovers we sold and I've found some information that I hope would be helpful.

"Great."

"Would you please pass on to Lieutenant Hunter that one of the silver Range Rovers was rented out to Alex Vannover on a Friday, the same Friday that the flight attendant was killed."

"Thank you Patti. We really appreciate you taking the time. Would you happen to have the license number?

Yes, I'll text it to you.

Thanks. I'll share that with Lt. Hunter; and if you would please, can you give me a call on this number if he rents with you again."

"Sure. No problem."

"Thanks."

~

Long Beach Police detectives awakened Rusty Adderly in his ground floor Travelodge unit, after having checked with the manager regarding his tenant's habits and reviewing video camera footage of the premises for the last 24 hours. Adderly had paid his rent on time, and kept his Harley chopper under a tarp in front of his motel unit next to a sky blue 1956 Chevy pickup he had restored to nearly concourse-grade condition.

The video showed that the Chevy stayed parked during the previous 24 hours, but his motorcycle was in and out of its parking stall throughout the day, and then remained parked from 10:15 PM until 7:34 AM, when detectives arrived at the motel. The detectives had learned from the manager that Adderly worked as a mechanic at an independent auto repair shop, and kept furniture and motorcycle parts in a small storage unit at a commercial lot while he saved for a home with a garage.

As he opened the door to his room, Adderly appeared to be suffering from a hangover, and was quite convincing in his look of surprise upon being contacted by the Long Beach Police detectives. Department of Justice records had revealed that he had a .38 caliber Smith & Wesson revolver registered to him, as well as a Remington 870 12 gauge shotgun. During a consent search of his room, the revolver was found in a holster, inside a drawer in a nightstand. He stated that the shotgun was locked up in his storage unit. A consent search of his Chevy pickup was like turning pages in a feature article in Hot Rod Magazine. It was as if fast food had never been taken home inside the cab. The interior looked and smelled new, and Adderly was clearly proud of the work he had performed in making the vehicle a show piece.

Upon hearing of Holmquist's murder, Adderly's reaction of sorrow seemed genuine, and his comments were those of concern for her children. When asked if he was open to providing a cotton swab of his mouth for DNA cell collection, he even willingly complied for later comparison with semen and fingernail scrapings. Despite their initial suspicion, the detectives could not find sufficient probable cause to arrest, and left the motel with a test tube containing their DNA sample and a couple photos of Adderly's truck, and headed back to the station.

~

The lunch hour left the Detective Bureau quiet, in contrast to the normal sounds of ringing phones, loud volume settings to the police radio, and the frequent conversations between work cubicles. But today Detective Bob Luther stayed seated at his desk, chewing his tuna sandwich, and piecing together a new homicide book that would include the lab reports, interview transcriptions, photographs, and investigative supplemental reports. The giant, 3-ring binder would eventually be filled with all the details of the story of the violent ending of the life of a Swedish immigrant mother.

Luther's focus was interrupted by a shadow cast across his desk. Chief Steinhoffer's body even blocked most of the sunlight shining through the windows facing the high rise buildings marking a pathway along Ocean Boulevard. Steinhoffer held a small piece of paper from his notepad imprinted with: "From the Desk of the Chief."

"Bob, I have a request. A friend of mine who's running for City Council was the victim of road rage while driving home from Orange County on the 405 Freeway."

Handing Luther the paper from his notepad, he continued:

"He wrote down the license number of the car, which I jotted down. The guy tried to run him off the road around Beach Boulevard, and he and his wife didn't know which agency should investigate it. Can you run the plate, find the registered owner, and then run a criminal history, or even a Lexis/Nexus to see what kind of litigation the suspect's been involved in?"

"Sure Chief, but for the criminal history, I should have a case number associated with the computer search. Beach Boulevard and the 405 is probably Huntington Beach Police, or even the CHP (California Highway Patrol) might be willing to take the report."

"Just run the search, give me the information, and I'll tell him what he needs to do to handle the situation. For goodness sake, I've got a law degree, Bob. I think I can address this issue appropriately."

"Not a problem, Sir. I was just thinking since it was for a friend, you might want to play it straight, in case of a DOJ audit."

"Take a Valium, Bob. I'm sure Dispatch runs criminal histories on car stops daily without worrying about the State coming down here with a hammer. I'll check back with you later. Thanks, Bob."

Chapter 41

Assembled in the Investigative Conference room, Hunter, Blackburn, Miller, and Winslow met to "white board" all the clues and evidence gathered to this point on the murders. Hunter opened:

"Victim #1, Kimberly Donahue, was killed by a .25 auto bullet fired into her head, and was dumped by the pepper tree on Old Barranca Road. The murder took place on a Friday night. Victim #2, Wendy Gilbert, was killed by a .25 auto bullet fired into her head, and was dumped at the same location. This murder also took place on a Friday night, and she was last seen riding in a silver Range Rover departing from the Airporter Hotel parking lot.

Blackburn rose from his seat, and approached the white board on the conference room wall, felt tip pen in hand, and wrote as he spoke:

"The night that Victim #2 was murdered, a Long Beach Police officer who formerly worked as a Sheriff's Special Deputy at John Wayne Airport, Alex Vannover, rented a silver Range Rover from Paragon Executive Coaches, located at the airport. The Range Rover has since been sold."

"Have we tracked down who bought that Range Rover?" Hunter asked, hoping to find Gilbert's DNA in the vehicle, thus tying Vannover to the crime.

"I've got the plate; I'll run a history on it after our meeting," added Blackburn.

"So, a white Range Rover previously rented by Vannover, was rented to a co-ed who crashed it on MacArthur Boulevard.

Inside the vehicle, two .25 auto shell casings were found, containing blood stains," Hunter added.

"The blood was analyzed as "A" positive, but there were no DNA hits in the system," Sgt. Miller interjected.

"Was the second murder on a Friday?" Hunter asked.

"Yes, and Vannover's days off when he worked for the Sheriff's Department were Wednesday, Thursday, and Friday's. Both of our victims were killed while Vannover still worked for the Sheriff," Blackburn added.

"What about Turk's? Wasn't Victim #1 seen at Turk's restaurant and bar the night she was murdered? Were we able to get the waitress to identify the guy she was with at Turk's?" Hunter asked.

"She said that she couldn't positively identify Vannover as the guy, based on the photo we showed her. It was his academy picture, and he had a buzz cut at the time." "And we've run guns registered to Vannover, and he does own a .25 caliber automatic, correct?" Hunter asked.

"He does," answered Blackburn

"How about the bartender at the Airporter, and Gilbert's flight attendant roommate? Did we show Vannover's photo to them, and try to get an I.D.?" Hunter asked.

"I'm trying to get a more recent photo of Vannover. I've asked my friend at Long Beach PD to see if he can get a swearing-in picture of him.

"With Vannover being hired so recently by Long Beach, what are the chances we can get access to the background they did on him?"

"Well Scott, my friend actually did the guy's background, but the Chief overruled his recommendation for not hiring him. The issue we've been dancing around is the fact that this subject we're looking at is the nephew of our previous Chief. We all know how difficult it was to work under him.

"What's your friend's name?"

"His name's Bob Luther; he's the robbery/homicide detective working the murder Long Beach just had."

"What's the connection Long Beach has with our two murders?"

"I spoke to Luther the day they discovered the homicide. He said he had seen our flyer, and the similarities were that the victim in each case was an attractive female with a .25 caliber gunshot to the head."

"Did he say that they had developed any connection to Vannover?"

"Luther told me they first suspected a guy who had just pled guilty to assaulting her, but he said that they had video evidence giving him an alibi."

"Where's this Vannover live? Do we have his work schedule?"

"He lives in Orange County, Costa Mesa. He's got the same days off as he had with the Sheriff – Wednesday, Thursday, and Friday. They're on a 4/10 plan."

"Well that's weird. The Long Beach murder was on his day off, Friday. Why would he drive up to Long Beach from the O.C. on his day off? And what about this Giroux guy?

"Luther told me he checked the work schedule, and Vannover worked an overtime shift on P.M.'s that Friday, Scott," Blackburn interjected.

Wasn't Giroux renting Rovers also? Janowitz filled out an F.I. (field interview card) on him sitting in a Range Rover with his girlfriend at the pepper tree. That needs to be explored a little further, or do you attribute that to chance, or coincidence?"

No, you're right Scott. That needs more work."

"Stephanie, can you take that one?"

"No problem, I'll take care of it, Lieutenant."

"Thanks, let's tighten things up and get these ladies some justice."

Chapter 42

Chief Daniel Steinhoffer was riveted to the chair at his desk, with the phone receiver glued to his left ear as his secretary screened the call from the front desk.

"Daniel, the front desk just called, and a reporter and camera crew for ABC News are in the lobby requesting an on-camera interview regarding the pursuit terminating spike strips the Department currently uses and endorses. What would you like me to tell them?"

"Tell them I'm in a meeting and schedule an appointment – for next week."

"They're going to want something a little sooner, more contemporaneous with the news."

"Exactly. Tell them I'm booked up until next week."

~

Ten minutes later, Chief Steinhoffer's secretary advised him the City Manager, Suzanne Duncan, was on the line.

"Hello Suzanne?"

"Yes, Daniel. Are you trying to pawn this on-camera hot seat interview onto me?"

"Of course not, I'm just being strategic, and pushing it off until it is no longer newsworthy."

"Well, they're in the City Hall lobby now, wanting to interview me for a mess you got us all into. Give them something that admits no wrongdoing. I want you to get out in front of this story – now."

~

"This is Jesse Garza, ABC News. Chief Steinhoffer, in light of the tragic death of the Kansas City police officer killed during the deployment of the R.C. Enterprises spike strips which your organization tested and endorsed, do you still stand behind the use of this product for terminating pursuits?"

"The Long Beach Police Department is working with the manufacturer and the Kansas City Police Department in ascertaining the cause of this tragic accident. If it is determined to be an engineering issue, the manufacturer has assured us that appropriate steps will be taken to correct any structural changes that need to be made in the product. If the cause is determined to be operator error, then we will examine the training protocols and promulgate to all agencies using this product additional training to ensure that proper deployment is consistently accomplished."

"Is it true that you are an investor in R.C. Enterprises?"

"R.C. Enterprises' CEO, Reuben Cohen, and I have been friends for many years, and I have been a strong supporter of the products he has developed which have promoted the safety of police officers as well as the public at large."

"Isn't it true that any litigation that R.C. Enterprises loses as a result of this tragedy could affect you financially, being an investor in this company?"

"I'm not going to speculate on any litigation that may or may not result from this incident. My only hope is that the officer's family is comforted during their mourning and time of great loss. Thank you."

~

"Hi Bob, Tom Blackburn with Irvine PD."

"Hi Tom, what's up?"

"Well, we're still working these two homicides, and we were round table discussing some of the similarities. Your officer, Alex Vannover, also your Chief's nephew, appears to have some troubling connections that we need to dig a little deeper on. First, does your Chief know we're even looking at him?"

"I don't think so; and we're not bringing it up. Nor have we discussed with him how there may be connections to our case. We want to be pretty sure before we stir that pot."

"Yeah, understand. I know that you did his nephew's background. Did you find anything when you checked with the Orange County Sheriff's Department?"

"I did find that Vannover had two complaints for soliciting dates from women that he contacted on duty. Based upon those, plus some comments regarding immaturity, I recommended to Steinhoffer that he not be hired. But Steinhoffer said that since the complainants wanted to remain anonymous, that he would not consider them credible, and he overruled my recommendation."

"Have you received any similar complaints since he started working for you guys?"

"I haven't checked. If there were any, they would either be found in Internal Affairs as a formal investigation, or they could be handled at the Patrol level, and documented in a file in the watch commander's office, and used for review purposes. If he has anything handled by I.A., since they report directly to the Chief, any inquiry by me would alert the Chief."

"OK, got it. I don't want to put you in any kind of compromising situation. But if you could check that watch commander file, that would be greatly appreciated. Also, would you know if any photos were taken of his swearing in ceremony? The photo I have of him was taken after his Sheriff's Academy graduation, and his hair was all buzzed off."

"Let me see what I can do about that watch commander file, and I'll check with our photographer regarding that swear-in, and get back to you."

"Thanks Bob. Any developments on your homicide case?"

"The husband identified the body; that was rough. But he said that his wife wore a diamond pendant around her neck all the time, and it was missing. It was three diamonds mounted vertically on a white gold bar, with a matching gold chain. It looks like her killer took a souvenir. Also, we recovered the .25 caliber slug that exited the back of her skull, and the flat base of the round had dried blood on it. The interesting part was that the DNA didn't match the victim's."

"Wow, that's interesting. We've recovered shell casings that we think may be associated with Vannover that had blood stains on them. We recovered them from a Range Rover he had rented before the vehicle was involved in an accident by the person who rented the car after him. Do you remember the blood type on your slug?"

"I think it's "A" but let me call you back with that."

"Sounds good, thanks Bob."

Chapter 43

The call went out as an injury traffic accident at the intersection of Olive Avenue and East 36th Street. Two vehicles were reported involved, with the driver of one lying in the street convulsing. An engine company with paramedics was dispatched along with a motor officer for traffic control, and a marked unit to take the report. Officer Alex Vannover arrived on scene, and found the Ford Taurus broadsided by a Dodge Pacifica. Several residents in the neighborhood stood on the sidewalk gawking while some attended to the driver lying in the street by covering him in blankets to control his body temperature from shock.

At 4:00 PM there was little traffic, but the sound of the crash drew a sizable crowd, despite the uncharacteristic blustery weather of the day. The heavy foliage of the large trunked trees shielded much of the sun that would have illuminated the stop sign on Olive. The skid marks and points of rest gave a primary collision factor as failure to stop for a posted stop sign by the driver of the Pacifica.

Vannover's first point of business after ensuring that the injured driver was attended to by the paramedics, was to gather the driver's licenses and vehicle registrations from both drivers. He then solicited witnesses from the crowd.

Out of the three people making themselves known, was a nineteen year old strawberry blonde cheerleader from Cal State Long Beach, who timidly raised her hand. Vannover approached her first with a warm smile. Tawnee Brookshire lived on the corner of E. 36th Street and Myrtle Avenue, and was finishing up her three mile run when she stopped at the corner of Olive, and seeing the Pacifica showing no indication of slowing.

Vannover was captivated by her athletic beauty, and struggled to jot coherent notes regarding her statement. He asked that she wait until he could get statements from the other witnesses.

The ambulance departed for the hospital, the engine company loaded up their gear, tow trucks removed the damaged vehicles from the intersection, and Vannover was still talking to Tawnee. She may have seemed reticent to raise her hand as a witness, but there was no doubt that she was open to Vannover's demonstrated interest in her.

Within a few days, a Long Beach police car was seen by neighbors on Tuesday around 4:00 p.m. parked in the alley behind the house located on the corner of Myrtle Avenue and East 36th Street. Tawnee's parents were at work until much later, and her last class ended at 3:00. Coincidentally, Vannover's swing shift patrol briefing ended on Tuesdays at 4:00.

It only took a few weeks before the routine was noticed by the city councilman living around the block on California Avenue. His call to the watch commander's office regarding the police activity in the alley was met with dismissal, until he advised the lieutenant that it was a regular event. This generated a response that the councilman's observations would be looked into, and if the activity was determined to be non-official business, appropriate action would be taken.

The call came from Dispatch to Vannover's call sign to contact the watch commander. Such calls were generally bad news and with most officers often created a variety of emotions, including worry, reflection, even terror as to what might have happened to warrant a complaint. Vannover, felt none of these emotions, all he thought he needed was a plan to formulate a credible defense.

Lieutenant Leonard suspected what was happening, but would await his officer's explanation.

168

"Alex, this is not a complaint, but more of an inquiry by a city councilman regarding the reason why your patrol car was seen on a regular basis in the alley behind his residence on California Avenue."

"Oh? Well, a couple weeks ago I handled an injury traffic accident at Olive Avenue and East 36th Street, and one of the witnesses was a nineteen year old gal who was jogging in the area. She saw one of the drivers lying in the street convulsing and suffering from shock. I took her statement, gave her my business card, and told her that if she could remember any additional details to give me a call. She called and said that she was having nightmares, and wanted to talk about it. So after swing shift briefing, I would take time to talk to her."

"You expect me to believe that Alex? I would bet that she's attractive, and likes young men in uniforms. Listen, you're exposing yourself and the department to some serious problems by your indiscretion. Give her a referral card for counseling services, and I'm ordering you to make no further contact with her while on duty, unless it's in an official call for service. Do you understand me?"

"Yep."

Chapter 44

At lunchtime, Chief Steinhoffer ventured into the Detective Bureau to ascertain the status of Luther's records search he had requested. However, on this day Luther had joined a birthday party for the Bureau's secretary at Bubba Gump's Shrimp restaurant. Steinhoffer used the opportunity to dig through Luther's desk to see if he could recognize anything related to the license plate he had given Luther regarding a prospective councilman's road rage incident.

What caught his attention was a photograph of the swearing in ceremony for several new officers which included Steinhoffer's nephew, Alex Vannover. Steinhoffer wondered what Luther's purpose was for the photo, and took a mental note to bring it up when he next met with him.

~

Following his marriage proposal, Hunter had marked the date on the calendar when Ashley would next be home for a weekend following a long stretch of consecutive days away from each other. They each still retained separate condos, but sometimes it was more convenient for Ashley to stay over at Hunter's Newport Back Bay home. He would pick her up at John Wayne Airport, and they would head straight to the Rusty Pelican for dinner at sunset overlooking Newport Bay.

Seeing her waiting curbside in her American Airlines uniform, he could tell that she was tired, and most likely suffering from jetlag. He needed to resort to Plan B if he had any hopes of salvaging this Friday on a short weekend. He pulled next to the curb, got out, and met her on the passenger side. He embraced her, they kissed, and he presented her with a single red rose, announcing to all those who were curbside that she was someone he loved.

While leaving the terminal, he handed her a chilled energy drink, and offered her the choice of the Rusty Pelican, or grabbing a pizza on the way back to his condo. Ashley chose the latter.

"How are the homicide cases coming along?"

"Looks like we have a third victim that might be related but this one happened in Long Beach."

"Really? How did she die? Was she taken to the pepper tree or found in Long Beach?"

"Small caliber gunshot wound, and she was dumped at an oilfield in Long Beach."

"How awful."

"Yeah, the scary part is we might be dealing with a bad cop as the suspect."

"You're kidding. Irvine? Long Beach?"

"It may be a Long Beach cop."

"How do they end up with someone so warped becoming a police officer?

"Even a psychopath can fool a police psychologist. And to top it off, the guy might be the nephew of the Chief."

"Steinhoffer?"

"Yep."

"I thought we were done with him when he left Irvine."

"I wish it were so."

"That man is horrible to deal with. I'll bet if it is his nephew, he'll try to put roadblocks in your investigation."

"He was that way even when cases didn't involve his family. But we're still not really certain the nephew is the suspect."

"Does he know you're looking at his nephew?"

"I don't think so. How was your flight?"

"Nice people, no crying babies."

By the time they had arrived in his garage, the energy drink had kicked in, the smell of the pizza had enveloped the interior of the car, and they were both more than ready to eat. Hunter's second story, 3-bedroom condominium, had a panoramic view of the Newport Back Bay nature preserve. The setting sun reflected off the water, into his family room, and drew them onto the balcony, where they sipped their Cabernet.

"I think I'll slip out of this flight attendant's outfit, and into something more comfortable."

"Remember how you once said that you had a fantasy about sex and uniforms, when you saw me in my dress blues?"

"Yeah."

"Well, can you leave that on for a few more minutes?"

"Sure."

Chapter 45

The five o'clock hour had come and gone, and Patti Nilsson's relief still hadn't arrived to take the evening shift at Paragon Executive Coaches. She was worried that something might be wrong, until she received a phone call from her relief saying that her car's battery had died, and Triple A had just left after jumping her car.

Sheriff's Special Deputy Larry Giroux had ended his shift, and arrived at the counter, asking to rent another Range Rover for the evening. Patti began completing the contract on her computer terminal, but was interrupted by her discovery that Giroux had rounded the corner, and was standing next to her on the opposite side of the counter. As he moved closer, rubbing his body next to hers, Patti stopped the transaction and told him to immediately get on the other side of the counter if he wanted to rent an SUV with her company.

Giroux pleaded that he thought that they were friends, and that he always had strong feelings for her. Patti reached for her cell phone and displayed it to him, stating that she had his supervisor's number on speed-dial. She then showed him her screen saver, which was a photo of her with her stepfather in an Orange County Sheriff's Department uniform.

"My step-dad is the captain in charge of Internal Affairs for the Sheriff's Department. The only way he would let me take this job was for me to have access to a sheriff's supervisor. You are way out of line Mr. Giroux. I don't know where you learned how to treat women, but if you continue on this path your career will end."

"Sorry, my mistake. I think I'll rent a Rover some other time. Just cancel the order."

He promptly left the rental car section, and the terminal. Patti's relief arrived shortly thereafter, and was warned of her encounter with Giroux for future reference.

~

The car stop was for expired registration, but Vannover could smell burnt marijuana inside the passenger compartment of the older model Toyota 4Runner. He called for a follow-up officer at northbound Atlantic Avenue, north of Cartegena, commonly referred to as the Bixby Knolls district. The driver and passenger were told to wait inside the vehicle while Vannover ran a records check on them both while awaiting assistance.

Officer Dennis Blair arrived within two minutes, and the driver and passenger were directed to the curb, where they were seated after a pat-down search for weapons. Blair stood by with them, while Vannover began a search of the vehicle for narcotics. During the search he found a small baggie of marijuana, approximately ½ ounce, in the glove compartment, and a small glass vial of cocaine in the center console. He also saw several loose rounds of 9mm hollow point ammunition scattered on the right rear passenger floorboard, but was unable to locate a firearm. The interior of the vehicle had several articles of clothing thrown about the seats and the trunk.

Vannover approached the driver, stood him up, and escorted him to the back passenger door of his police cruiser. He conducted a second, more detailed search for narcotics on the driver's person, and then placed handcuffs on him, before seating him in the back seat "cage" of the patrol car. Vannover called to Blair, "H&S, plus ammo," signaling that he had found Health & Safety Code violations, pertaining to narcotics and ammunition.

Vannover asked the driver where the pistol was within the vehicle, but was told that he didn't know. Vannover then

176

withdrew his Taser from its holster, displayed it in front of the driver's face, and removed the cartridges containing the barbed darts. He then pulled the trigger, causing the probes in the empty cartridge bays to arch with a bright blue bolt of electricity, creating a loud electrical pop. Vannover told the driver that he would run the charge into his thigh, if he did not tell him where the firearm was located.

The driver remained silent. Vannover waited until traffic began moving from the signal at Carson and Atlantic past his patrol car, making engine noise, then discreetly pushed the barrel end of the Taser against the driver's thigh. Before Vannover could pull the trigger, the driver yelled out, "It's in the jack compartment, behind the right rear wheel well."

Vannover holstered his Taser, closed the rear door of the patrol car, and opened the hatchback of the 4Runner. After clearing a pile of clothes, he opened the jack compartment, and retrieved a Browning Hi-Power 9mm pistol. After unloading it, he searched the passenger again for narcotics, and handcuffed him. He placed him in the back of the patrol car, and called a tow truck for vehicle storage. The driver told Vannover that the dope was his, but the passenger remained silent.

Although the 4Runner was registered to the driver, the firearm was registered to the passenger. Vannover arrested the driver for possession of narcotics, and the passenger for possession of a loaded firearm in public. The driver was booked, but the passenger was given a citation and released at the station.

Troubled by what he perceived as Vannover possibly torturing a suspect into an admission or confession, Officer Blair contacted his sergeant in the field to share his observations. During the booking process, Sergeant Paul Washington attempted to speak with the driver regarding Blair's allegations, but the driver declined to discuss the alleged incident. Sgt. Washington directed the booking jailer to have the driver remove his pants.

177

Washington observed that there were no electrical burn marks on his thigh.

Sergeant Washington then called Vannover into the watch commander's office.

"Did you threaten your arrestee with your Taser to get him to tell you where the gun was hidden?"

"No, is that what he told you?"

"Who told me is not important. I want you to tell me how you found the gun."

"Are you accusing me of a crime?"

"Are we going down that road? OK, I'll read you your rights under Miranda, in compliance with the California Peace Officers' Bill of Rights."

Washington pulled out his Miranda card, and read Vannover his constitutional rights.

"With these rights in mind, are you willing to talk to me?"

"Sure."

"OK, did you use your Taser to compel a suspect to reveal where a firearm was hidden in a car that you stopped tonight?"

"No."

"Did you threaten a suspect with your Taser to reveal where a firearm was hidden in a car that you stopped tonight?"

"No."

"All right. I'm going to turn this matter over to Internal Affairs, and let them investigate what happened on your car stop. You're dismissed."

Chapter 46

It was the third suicide on railroad tracks in two months, warranting a Detective Bureau call-out. This time it was the stretch of track between Culver Drive and Jeffrey Road, that ran parallel to the villages of Greentree to the north, and Deerfield to the south. A nineteen year old man sat on the tracks in front of a 65 mile per hour, northbound AmTrak Surfliner.

The bulk of the man's body was thrown south of the tracks, toward Culver Drive, but numerous dismembered body parts were scattered for several yards on both sides of the north and southbound tracks. CSI technicians and coroner personnel worked quickly to photo and mark positions, so that removal could be hastened to prevent children departing the schools in Deerfield from viewing the gruesome scene.

Blackburn and Winslow arrived first, followed by Hunter and Miller. Despite the engineer seeing the deceased on the tracks as far away as Jeffrey, the train couldn't stop until approximately ¼ mile past the point of impact. As soon as the engineer and conductor were interviewed, and the engine processed by CSI, the train was sent forward toward its destination. Surprisingly, only one person witnessed the actual impact. A 64 year old retiree walking his dog along the cement path traversing the tracks watched the man walk through the opening in the block wall enclosing Greentree, and calmly sit on the tracks, facing away from the approaching train.

Blackburn and Winslow had already begun backgrounding the deceased, and learned he was a sophomore at Chapman University with a declared major in political science. His parents resided in Irvine, but his own apartment was in the City of

Orange, near the university. Hunter checked in with Blackburn for an update.

"This is a mess, Tom. I just can't imagine someone sitting there calmly and feeling the vibrating track rapidly shaking violently until impact. Is there anything common to the two previous incidents?"

"They were all males, roughly the same age within two years. The times were different, so they were struck by either the AmTrak trains, or the MetroLink commuters. The first one happened at Sand Canyon, near the Irvine Country Store. The guy walked under the automatic arms and stepped in front of a speeding AmTrak locomotive. The second one happened at Culver Drive, where the deceased jumped in front of the MetroLink commuter train. Each of the victims had tattoos of the five-pointed, pentagram star on their left forearms."

"Well that's interesting. Didn't we run into that marking on a homicide?"

"Yep, that "burning astronaut" caper on Ridgeline and Turtle Rock, which we handed over to Costa Mesa PD. But his pentagram was on the ground below him, and used as a reservoir for gasoline."

"Do we have anything tying some Satanist activity in the city?"

"Not yet. We don't do press releases on suicides. Do you want to make an exception, and see if the public has anything to offer?"

"No, I'm not ready to tie up our phone lines on this while we're still looking for clues on the homicides. Let's just put it out at Neighborhood Watch meetings, and see if any Watch Captains have heard anything."

Chapter 47

As a result of a promotion, a vacancy on the Special Weapons and Tactics Team (SWAT) became available, and in light of Hunter's experience on the team, he was asked to sit on the interview panel to select one of twelve applicants. He looked forward to a break from the pressures of the homicides, which his team could cover for the day; and he would have the opportunity of interviewing the department's best. To arrive at the interview stage, the twelve being examined would have passed a physical agility test, a firearms qualification, and 2-3 scenarios involving actors with decision making.

Today's panel with Hunter included the lieutenant in charge of the team, and two of the sergeant team leaders. The interviews were conducted in the Detective Conference Room, and participants were to appear in either Class A uniforms, or coat and tie. The experience level of the applicants testing today ranged from three to six years. Although it was previously allowed to be in assignments such as Detectives, Traffic, or Training, this list of candidates could not be assigned to any other division except Patrol, due to the amount of training required.

The interview questions would cover motivation for applying, qualifications for selection, an ethical problem, and a stressful tactical decision. Hunter was hoping that his exchanges with the interviewees would restore some of his faith in the character of his fellow brothers in law enforcement. The stories developing around those officers that his team was beginning to examine in relation to these homicides were reflecting weaknesses in the hiring process. Whether they were management or line level, the methods for selection were missing a means of identifying character.

For SWAT, the character component would present to the applicant a scenario that, on occasion, occurs in the field and creates an ethical dilemma:

Two patrol officers in separate vehicles are dispatched to a silent burglar alarm at an industrial company during the evening hours. The primary assigned officer arrives first, and observes that the business deals with the recycling of scrap metal, which has become profitable to black market thieves. The front of the building has a glass front door to the lobby and offices, with several windows. To check the back doors, officers would have to scale a nearly six foot block wall to gain access to the back side of the building and check the storage yard for any intrusions. During the past month, the business has had a series of false alarms.

The primary officer checks the front door and windows, and sees no evidence of a burglary having been attempted. The back-up officer arrives, and asks if the primary officer has already checked the perimeter of the business. The primary officer states that he has already checked it. The back-up officer knows that just one week ago, the department conducted semi-annual training, and that one of the scenarios required officers to scale a five foot fence, and then once on the other side, draw his or her firearm and fire six rounds into a silhouette target. The back-up officer further knows that the primary officer has gained weight, and was unable to scale the five foot fence during the training exercise. What action, if any, would you as the back-up officer take to complete this call for service?

The best response of the day was given by a former Marine Corps corporal, and previous member of the Corps' Force Recon:

"I would tell the primary officer, that I would make a quick extra check of the back to make sure that we didn't miss anything, and jump the block wall myself, after telling the primary officer to turn the volume on his radio up, in the event that I needed help. I would check the rear of the building for intrusions, and if none were found, jump back over the wall and clear the call."

"I would then radio a request to meet my supervisor, and recount for him or her, the previous scenario. I would say that I do not want to call another officer a liar, but I couldn't confidently clear that call, knowing that my observations from the previous week would suggest that my partner officer probably could not have physically performed the task required to ensure that that business was secure."

Members of the SWAT team are initially placed on a probationary status until they have graduated from a certified SWAT academy, and have been a member of the team for six months. They are monitored closely, and their targets on the range are verified by supervision. When a team member shows up on a call before the arrival of a supervisor, officers frequently look toward that team member for leadership. Team members often place within the top three on promotional lists for sergeant, based upon their demonstrated leadership skills.

Although the day was mentally taxing, Hunter was proud of the candidates who tested for the vacancy, and were placed on the eligibility list. He hoped that he would have his homicide cases closed and the suspect sentenced before today's top scoring candidate received his golden eagle SWAT uniform pin.

Chapter 48

It wasn't long before a Neighborhood Watch Captain heard information from a resident regarding pentagrams and the suicides on the railroad tracks, and a clue was soon forwarded to their Crossroads Policing Area officer. The city is divided into three geographic policing districts: Portola to the north, University to the south, and Crossroads in the central area. An Irvine housewife had reported that her middle school aged son and his friend walked through the fence separating the Marine Corps Helicopter Base from Harvard Avenue. The boys found that one of the abandoned outbuildings had multiple satanic drawings and paintings on the walls inside, and it appeared that some type of ritual had been conducted.

Like its neighbor, the former El Toro Marine Corps Air Base, the helicopter station, located in the Tustin city limits, had been scheduled for closure next year. Originally used for servicing military blimps, the Tustin "Lighter-Than-Air" Base (LTA) was situated on the northwest border of the City of Irvine. Home of the world's largest wooden structures, the Marine Base was built around two mammoth wooden blimp hangars, and a red and white checkered control tower. With the demise of military blimps, the base was then converted for servicing Marine Corps helicopters.

The buildings and short runways were used in the filming of scenes from the movie, "Pearl Harbor." The famous Jimmy Doolittle raid over Tokyo which was practiced on land before being launched from aircraft carriers was re-enacted on the Tustin base with B-25 light bombers flying over the College Park Village in Irvine.

One of the outbuildings on land no longer in use by the Marines had apparently been occasionally occupied by Satan worshippers. It was possible that the pentagram tattoos found on the railroad track suicide victims were related to the images in the small, shack-like buildings, but first the teens' observations needed to be corroborated.

Working the swing shift in the Crossroads Policing Area, Officer Jim Janowitz received the call from the watch commander's office to make contact with the residents in College Park, and have the son point out the building in which he and his friend had discovered the satanic artwork. Upon arrival, Janowitz drove southbound along Harvard Avenue with the middle schooler, who identified the break in the fence where he had entered the open field leading to the outbuilding. Janowitz dropped him off at home, and then requested a back-up officer meet him at the College Park baseball fields.

Both officers met, and then parked their patrol units southbound on Harvard, by the fence break and stood by their vehicles. The sun was just starting to set, with the bottom edge of the golden orb touching the top of the wooden blimp hangar. A slight Santa Ana wind blew the waist high grass on the open field, as Janowitz pointed the route that they would take to reach 10' X 12' corrugated metal shed which the boy had identified.

Slowly tracking through the grass, they arrived, and posted up on each side of the unlocked door. They withdrew their Sig Sauer .45 caliber pistols with weapon mounted lights from their holsters, and announced their presence. Janowitz crisscrossed in from the hinge side, while his partner followed, covering his blind side. Their lights flashed across the walls, covering fields of fire, but found the structure empty.

Janowitz drew his standard size flashlight from his sap pocket as they holstered their pistols. The four walls were covered with ornate murals of acrylic paint in shades of black, purple, and fiery red and orange. The figures included rudimentary scenes from Dante's Inferno, Disney's Fantasia's Devil scenes from "Night on Bald Mountain," and several pentagrams and ram's heads.

Janowitz recognized crude tattoo needles similar to those found in the jails, which consisted of a needle jammed into the end of a toothbrush handle, and melted into place. Empty ink wells were on a table, and there appeared to be a small stone altar on the floor charred with soot.

After taking photographs, they returned to their patrol cars and put themselves back in service. Janowitz phoned Hunter with their findings:

"Based on your observations, Jim, could you tell how recently someone had visited the shack?"

"Well, some of the artwork wasn't quite finished, and there were some fast food wrappers there that still had some food attached to it. So, I'm assuming that if it had been there long, the ants would have eaten the scraps. I think a couple days ago, probably someone was there."

"OK Thanks Jim. I think we'll assign the Narc's to stake the place out."

Chapter 49

The first order of business for Tuesday morning was for Hunter to turn in his Crown Victoria staff car for vehicle changeover. Irvine's fleet of patrol cars and command staff vehicles were leased rather than purchased. Patrol units were rotated out of service every two years, and staff vehicles every four years. The motor pool technicians had set aside for Hunter a new graphite colored Ford Crown Victoria with code 3 red lights and siren hidden within the grille, and strobe lights in the backs of the side view mirrors. His old car would be stripped and sent out to the dealership to be wholesaled.

Hunter headed upstairs to his office while some of the equipment from his old car, such as a shotgun mount and a trunk storage vault, were transferred to his new "Crown Vic." Before he could finish reading the 24 hour log, Hunter saw Bob, the motor pool technician, standing in his overalls at the threshold of Hunter's office holding a garage door opener.

"Sorry to interrupt, Boss, but we found this garage door opener under the seat of your old staff car and thought you might have forgotten it."

Hunter looked with puzzlement at the rectangular shaped, black plastic opener held in the technician's right hand.

"Thanks "Bob," but I've got a Sears garage door opener for my house, and it's a smaller device that clips to my sun visor. That's not mine. Where did you find that?"

"It was under the driver's seat of your car, Boss"

"Thanks Bob, I'll try to track down who it belongs to."

Hunter held the device, turned it over, and studied its markings. It was an older model Black & Decker with a black strip of Dymo tape with the initials "S.D." over the battery cover. He couldn't remember having seen it before. He tried to remember if he'd ever loaned his car to anyone. It was then that he realized that Chief Steinhoffer had borrowed it during the three month period Hunter attended the FBI National Academy in Quantico, Virginia.

The FBI National Academy is a semester long course of study, designed by J. Edgar Hoover as a leadership school for prospective chiefs of police. Candidates must be of the rank of lieutenant or higher, receive the recommendation of their chief, and pass a background check and physical exam. The entire program was designed to improve the professionalism of law enforcement command staff, and ensure the cooperation of local authorities when the FBI conducts investigations in local jurisdictions.

The time of Hunter's absence must have worked to Steinhoffer's advantage when he was in need of a car while his new staff vehicle was being ordered. Hunter and others within the command staff had suspected Steinhoffer of having a romantic relationship with the city manager at that time. Maybe S.D. stood for Suzanne Duncan, and Steinhoffer had been given her garage door opener to enable him to have access to her condominium. Hunter chuckled to himself at the prospect of showing Steinhoffer the garage door opener the next time he saw him.

~

The first Tuesday evening of the month Chief Steinhoffer and City Manager Suzanne Duncan sat in their respective seats at the scheduled City Council meeting. Throughout the meeting each discreetly exchanged glances with one another in anticipation of another romantic tryst. Although Dr. O'Connell was giving another out of town seminar, the Chief's status was still rocky following his mishandling of the spike strip fiasco. He would have to wait and see whether his luck had taken a better turn.

Officer Alex Vannover kept track of his aunt's lecture schedule and anticipated that there could be trouble afoot involving her wayward husband. Vannover impatiently waited for his partner to speed up this 5150 call (mental patient) so he could get off work on time. But, unfortunately, this particular poor bipolar schizophrenic seemed to be experiencing some hallucinations, and Vannover's partner didn't seem to have a solution to wrapping up the guy's story about his visions of little men entering his home through a crack in the ceiling.

Vannover remembered hearing from several department veterans that a radar speed gun could have more applications than just the recording of speed limit violations. So he ran out to his patrol car, retrieved the radar device, brought it into the man's living room, fired the gun at the ceiling crack and announced that the little men were now magnetized and unable to fit through the opening in the plaster. They were then quickly able to jump in the car and head to the station.

Leaving the locker room, Vannover was relieved to see Steinhoffer's staff car was still in the parking lot and he climbed into the cab of his pickup and moved to a position where he could stakeout the chief without detection while awaiting his departure. Once again, Vannover followed the chief to the MacArthur Boulevard off ramp and waited to see if he would continue southbound on the 405 Freeway, or exit MacArthur, and follow his baser nature. As expected, the chief chose the latter.

Vannover tracked him to Duncan's Newport Beach condo, and was thoroughly disgusted. He resolved to develop a strategy to address the situation.

Chapter 50

"Tom, Bob Luther here with Long Beach PD."

"Hey Bob, you solve your body dump yet?"

"Nah, but I just wanted to get back to you on the blood type on the .25 caliber slug in our case. It was A positive as I suspected. I think I mentioned that we have no CODIS (DNA) hits, but the DNA on the slug matches the semen DNA. I did check the watch commander's files, and there're no complaints so far on Vannover."

"OK, thanks, still waiting on DNA from our end also. How about that swear-in photo?"

"Oh yeah, I've got one on my desk. It might work for you. It's not full face, like a mug photo, but I can email you a jpeg."

"That'd be great. We'll give it a try. Thanks."

~

They sat motionless in the tall grass, waiting for their eyes to become accustomed to the darkness. Chuck Richards and Blake James were a team, not only partners in the Narcotics Unit, but also a sniper team on SWAT that consisted of a primary sniper and an observer. Both could function as snipers in a barricade, but tonight they were both observers assigned to gather intelligence on a vacant, former military structure suspected of being home to a satanic cult.

Their goal was securing information and avoiding detection. In their seated positions, wearing ghillie suits, they blended in with the acres of tall grass extending a few inches above their heads. Any movement was made incrementally, causing little disruption to their surroundings.

Around 8:15 PM, a human silhouette, barely visible in the clouded moonlight, could be seen walking from a car parked in the lot for the ballfields across the grass toward the radar shack. Richards grabbed his night vision camera to memorialize the trespass onto military land.

The subject, apparently a male, entered the shack carrying a backpack, and soon left with the pack showing less bulk than when first observed outside the structure. James keyed his pack-set radio requesting Dispatch assign two units to intercept the subject before he could reach his vehicle. Units 39-Delta 31, and 41 acknowledged and responded.

The two Delta shift officers detained the subject when he reached the parking lot, and began the interview process of filling out the F.I. (field interview) card, while Richards and James discreetly worked their way back to their van, where they doffed their ghillie suits. The sniper team then drove to the ballfield parking lot to conduct their interrogation.

"I'm Detective Richards, and this is my partner, Detective James. Your name is Rudy Paladino?"

"Yes sir," Paladino replied shaking convulsively.

"You're 19 years old. Is that correct?"

"Yes sir."

Richards sized him up – an emaciated doper, brain nearly fried from chronic drug use, following some cult, and willing to say anything to get himself out of a jam. If he was under the influence, it was hard to tell whether he was, or if drugs had taken a permanent toll.

"What's the significance of that tattoo on your left forearm?"

"Oh, that's just a 5-pointed star, symbolizing an astronomy club I belong to."

"Bullshit. That's a pentagram, and you're lying. I'm going to have the security guard for the base you were just walking across, come here, and we're going to arrest you for trespassing. Do you have a record? We're running your name right now."

"Yes, I'm on probation for shoplifting."

"What were you shoplifting?"

"Diapers, I sell them at the swap meet. The money pays for my ecstasy."

"One of the conditions of probation is that you break no laws. I'm assuming that a trespass arrest will violate your probation, and you can be sent to the Orange County Jail."

"Yes sir."

"O.K., here's what we're gonna do. You're going to answer all our questions truthfully, and we might let you go. If you lie, it's jail time."

"Do you understand?"

"Yes sir."

"You're in a satanic cult that meets at that vacant shack on the base. Correct?"

"Yes sir."

"How long have you been meeting here?"

"Nine months."

"How many people meet here?"

"About ten."

"What kind of sacrifices are you making on that small altar in the shack?"

"Small animals, cats, rabbits, squirrels."

"Who is the leader of this cult?"

"A guy named Carlos Baltazar."

"Where does he live?"

"Some place in Costa Mesa. He's a house painter, but we meet in a homeless encampment in the flood control channel near Angel Stadium sometimes."

"What's the deal with the suicides on the railroad tracks?"

"We have to bring Carlos money, narcotics, or a small animal to sacrifice. If we come emptyhanded, he will hand you a drug, tell you to take it, and he orders you to make an ultimate sacrifice on the tracks."

"How does he have that kind of control over you guys?"

"Carlos has tremendous power. But, I think the drug he gives might be LSD."

"What's going on with the body dumps by the pepper tree on Barranca Road?"

"I don't know anything about body dumps or a tree."

"Has Carlos done time in prison?"

"I think he was in Vacaville for killing somebody when he was young. You're not going to tell him I spoke to you, are you?"

"Don't give us a reason."

Rudy Paladino was sent on his way, after a photograph of him was taken, and sufficient information was obtained to complete an internal intelligence report. A summary of Paladino's interview was forwarded to Hunter, and Sgt. Miller alerted Costa Mesa Police concerning their resident satanic cult leader. Days of the week and times of meetings were recorded to establish an operational plan to build a case for the arrest of Baltazar for suspicion of murder, animal cruelty, and narcotics violations.

Chapter 51

Bob Luther was dreading this moment because he knew that it would be argumentative. The chief had asked him to research a license plate number associated with a road rage incident involving a possible candidate for the City Council. Compounding the issue was the fact that the candidate was a friend of the chief's, and the difficulty with interfacing with him was that his nephew was being looked at by another agency regarding a murder case.

Luther didn't want to ruin Irvine's case by having his chief possibly interfere and he worried that his own case could be compromised by a chief executive who had demonstrated his propensity to be protective of his relative of questionable character. He tried to time his visit to the corner office just before lunch, hoping that the meeting would be cut short.

"Good morning, Chief, I've got that information you requested on that plate. Here, I've written down the registered owner, where he lives, his mortgage holder, and his driving record. He has no outstanding warrants, and no criminal record. The title to his car is held by a teachers' credit union. Either he or his wife could be a teacher or government worker. His name is unusual and sounded familiar. On a hunch I checked the Medical Board of California, and the registered owner of the vehicle is a licensed ear, nose, and throat physician. Would there be anything else, sir?"

"Yes, I happened by your desk the other day and saw a photograph of the swearing-in ceremony for my nephew and some of our other new officers. Was there any particular reason why you needed that photo?"

"Well, Irvine PD had requested a photo of your nephew for elimination purposes on a case they were working, but I don't think that the photo is large enough to be reliable."

"What kind of crime were they trying to eliminate him as being involved in?"

"I believe it was a homicide, sir."

"Have you sent it yet?"

"Yes sir."

"Why didn't you contact me first? Didn't you think that I would have an interest in that kind of information?"

"Well, Chief, we didn't want to get you alarmed over something that may not be substantiated."

"From now on I want you, and anyone associated with this Irvine case to run everything by me before you send it to Irvine. Is that clear?"

"Crystal."

"What do you know about their case?"

"It's two female body dumps at the same Irvine location."

"What is the linkage with my nephew?"

"The suspect in one of the homicides claimed to be a cop, and rented a Range Rover. Your nephew rents Range Rovers."

"Sounds pretty thin to me."

"Well then, your nephew should have nothing to worry about."

"I'm not sure I have such confidence in the detective personnel with my former agency."

"They seem pretty squared away to me, sir. And the lead detective is a friend of mine."

"That's good to know. Like I said, everything gets run by me."

~

Luther realized that he needed to interview Vannover regarding his prior contact with the victim of their own body

198

dump, before his chief got to his nephew. He decided he would contact him immediately after today's swing shift briefing was dismissed.

"Good afternoon, Alex. Can I get you a glass of water?"

"No thanks."

"Alex, I've just got a few background questions I need to ask you about Lena Holmquist, our homicide victim from the oil field. I've read the arrest report you wrote for the truck driver you arrested for sexual battery. Had you ever had any prior contact with Holmquist before that evening at the 322 Café?"

"No."

"Did you have any contact with her following that night?"

"No."

"What do you remember about her?"

"She was pretty intoxicated, a little disheveled. She was angry, and definitely wanted Adderly arrested. She also wanted to stay and continue drinking, but we suggested that she take a cab home.

"Did you ever check back to see if she returned to the 322 Café that evening?"

"No, we saw her get into the cab, but never checked back to see if she returned that night to the café."

"Now, you worked your shift the night she was murdered, correct?"

"Yes."

"Did you have any calls to, or conduct any bar checks of the 322 Café that evening?"

"No."

"What route do you take home when you leave work?"

"Am I now a suspect in her killing?"

"No, I just thought that maybe you might have passed by the café, or the route she might have taken when she left there, and could have possibly seen something or someone suspicious in the area."

"I leave the station lot and catch the 710 Freeway off Shoreline Drive."

"Do you drive down First Street to get there?"

"No, that's the opposite direction."

"Did you drive your pickup truck to work the night of her murder?"

"I always drive it to work."

"Do you have any idea who might have committed her murder?"

"Well, did you check with Adderly, the guy who I arrested for assaulting her?"

"Yes, and he had an alibi."

"Then I would have no idea who would want to kill her. Did you check on her husband?"

"Yes, but based upon her time of death, it would appear that he was at home."

"Sounds like a real who-done-it."

Chapter 52

Wednesday began with another overcast morning, especially by the beach, where the fog was estimated to burn off about noon. It was Vannover's day off, but today he was on a mission. He had some surveillance to perform in preparation for his operation relating to his uncle.

While Vannover was planning his next move, Suzanne Duncan left her Newport Beach condo, heading in to work for an 8:00 AM staff meeting and she needed to stick to the agenda because she would have to return home for a 10:30 appointment for an estimate to install plantation shutters to replace her aging curtains.

In preparation for his operation, Vannover had purchased a set of blue overalls and a matching ball cap for his disguise as a maintenance man, and would bring a lightweight tool belt to finish off an authentic look. He waited until rush hour traffic had dissipated, and casually proceeded to Newport Beach in his Chevy Silverado pickup. His destination was Villa Point Drive, where he would scout the condominium of his uncle's paramour.

For Vannover, this was an essential element of his personal system of justice. For all that his aunt had done in protecting him and supporting his upbringing, it was necessary for him to eliminate any obstacle that might interfere in her happiness. And at this point that obstacle was Suzanne Duncan, the object of his uncle's affection, a man for whom he held little regard. This morning's mission would focus on gate access, door security, window hardware, and escape options.

He watched how long the exterior automobile gate took before its return cycle initiated, following the passage of a single vehicle. There appeared to be sufficient time for a second car to enter after the first vehicle passed, but the second would need to be within inches of the first's rear bumper. He decided against parking inside the gate, thinking he might have to wait for a vehicle ahead of him, in the event of a hasty exit. Instead, he decided he would park outside the gate and walk in following an entering car.

He knew the electronic door leading to the lobby and elevators could be enabled by a resident activating a buzzer from their residence, after calling on the intercom. However, he also knew he couldn't count on something as obvious as trying to follow an actual resident in. Looking for an alternative, he found a more discreet entrance at the ground level door leading to the stairwell. The spring in the latch assembly failed to throw the latch bolt completely into the strike plate and the door wasn't locking after exiting, leaving it ajar unless pushed by hand.

Duncan's condo unit was on the third floor with a view of the bay. A grappling hook to her balcony would be too noisy. He would need to check her front door lock for a credit card pry of the latch bolt. Vannover ascended the stairwell to her floor, and walked down the hallway to her door. He was in luck. She'd forgotten to throw the deadbolt.

As an enhancement to the image he was attempting to create with the Range Rover rentals, Vannover had opened an account with one of the few companies offering a metal credit card. He withdrew it from his wallet, and then pushed his shoulder into the center of the door while inserting the card into the small gap between the latch bolt and the strike plate, and pushed the door open. He entered and quickly walked into each room to mentally draft the floorplan. He checked the balcony and slider, then realized that the front door was moving.

Alarmed by the unsecured condition of her door, Suzanne Duncan entered tentatively, and immediately caught a glimpse of a man clad in blue overalls scaling over the railing of her balcony and vanishing out of sight. She screamed, then immediately stepped back into the hallway to grab her cellphone that had been tossed from her purse when she dropped it to the floor. She dialed 9-1-1 as she ran to her balcony to see if she could find where the intruder had gone.

In an effort to avoid Duncan seeing him, Vannover had landed on the balcony to the second floor condo units, and then dropped one more level, to the soft grass of the greenbelt landscaping. Seeing him, Duncan yelled to a nearby groundskeeper below to stop the fleeing intruder, but was met with a puzzled stare, possibly resulting from a language barrier.

By then, the Newport Beach Police 9-1-1 dispatcher had answered Duncan's call, and dispatched two units for an area search and crime report. By now, Vannover had fled the condo complex and was northbound on Jamboree Road heading home. When he reached the freeway, he began to worry that someone might have seen his truck leaving the scene and even possibly written down his license plate number.

To cover his tracks, Vannover drove his truck to the massive parking lot for the South Coast Plaza shopping mall and parked it near Macy's. He then walked the quarter mile home to his apartment and promptly phoned the Costa Mesa Police Department to report his pickup truck as being stolen.

Chapter 53

Suzanne Duncan called Chief Steinhoffer while awaiting the arrival of a Newport Beach police officer to take her burglary report. He was frustrated that she could not provide a useful description of the suspect, nor a license plate number for him to run. She told him she would call him back after speaking with the Newport officer.

Officer Steve Fonseca arrived, fresh off probation, and enthusiastic to work in a city known for its expensive real estate, and raucous July 4th beach parties. Unaware of Duncan's position and background, he began to lecture her on the importance of throwing deadbolts, and considering alarm systems, as she rolled her eyes impatiently. When she asked him how long she would need to wait for CSI, using his most authoritative voice he told her that he was unable to see any latent prints requiring a response by the Crime Scene Investigation Unit.

"Look Sherlock, I'm the city manager for the City of Long Beach, and the former city manager for Irvine. I've approved budgets for CSI units when DNA meant "Does Not Apply." "The reason you didn't see any latent prints is because they're "latent;" you can't see them until you dust for prints, you idiot."

"Sorry Ma'am, Fonseca said, hoping she wouldn't notice his red face," I'll have them out here within 20 minutes."

Realizing that he'd better try to make up for how that conversation had ended up, Officer Fonseca immediately checked with property management to determine if there were any video cameras on the premises that might have captured the suspect's description, or even a vehicle.

The rookie officer was relieved to find that the apparent intruder had missed a small camera with a wide angle lens near the vehicle entrance gate. Fonseca had the property manager play back the recording and discovered a man dressed in the overalls described by Duncan, entering a Chevy pickup truck parked near the gate. The resolution on the man's face was not very clear, but the letters on the front license plate to the pickup truck the man entered were sufficiently legible.

Fonseca ran the plate through the system and discovered that the registration information was confidential to the Long Beach Police Department, meaning that the owner was a police officer for that department and was allowed to hide personal information such as a home address to protect themselves and their families. Fonseca also discovered that shortly after the time of the reported burglary to Duncan's condo, the truck was reported as stolen.

Fonseca notified his supervisor of his findings, and he, in turn, contacted their department's internal affairs bureau. The lieutenant for the Newport Beach Police Department's internal affairs bureau then contacted Betsy Throckmorten, lieutenant in charge of internal affairs for the Long Beach Police Department. Throckmorten then met with Steinhoffer.

"Good morning, Chief, I have a sensitive issue to discuss with you. I was just contacted by Newport Beach PD's internal affairs lieutenant who said that Suzanne Duncan interrupted a burglary to her condo in Newport Beach this morning."

"Really? Was she hurt?"

"No, the suspect ran away. But there's video footage showing the burglar leaving the scene in a pickup truck registered to your nephew, Alex Vannover. But a short time after the burglary was reported, your nephew's truck was reported as stolen to the Costa Mesa Police Department."

"Does the man in the video look like my nephew?"

"It's not clear enough to make a facial recognition, but the build could be viewed as similar. However the suspect was wearing blue maintenance-type overalls, making it difficult to be certain."

"Have you spoken with Alex?"

"No, but I needed to talk with you about another matter with him concerning a car stop that he made. It seems that his follow-up officer believed that Alex may have used his Taser to induce a driver to tell him where a gun was located inside the vehicle."

"Did his follow-up officer actually see this? Is there any physical evidence?"

"Well, no, and the driver he pulled over refused to talk about it to Sgt. Washington."

"OK, let's hold off on that complaint for now. Let me try to get ahold of Alex, and find out some more information regarding the theft of his truck."

"I can handle that if you'd like me to Sir."

"That's OK, Betsy, I'm curious about his truck. I'll let you know what he says about it."

~

"Alex, this is your Uncle Daniel. What's this business I hear that your pickup truck was stolen?"

"How'd you hear about that?"

"That doesn't matter. I want to know the details."

"Well, there's not that much to it. I came out this morning and it was gone."

"Did you know that Suzanne Duncan's condo was broken into also this morning?"

"Really? What a bummer. Is she OK?"

"Do you know anything about it?"

"How would I know anything about it?"

"You and I need to have a talk. I want you in my office today. There're some things that just aren't adding up. How soon can you be here?"

"Well, it's my day off, and I don't have my truck."

"Rent something. You don't seem to have any reluctance in renting Range Rovers."

"Where'd you hear that?"

"Where I get my information is my own business. I want you in my office today before 5:00 pm."

Chapter 54

Most officers called into the chief's office would don their uniform to present a good impression for what might be a stressful encounter with the man in charge. But Vannover took liberties. Dressed in blue jeans, polo shirt, and sandals, Vannover decided that this look would be more appropriate, since he was the chief's relative.

"The city manager reported that she interrupted a burglary to her condo, and within an hour of her reporting it, you tell Costa Mesa PD that your pickup truck is stolen. You know how often we get reports of stolen vehicles following hit and runs, don't you. Most of the time they're bogus theft reports."

"Are you saying I made up my truck being stolen?"

"I'm saying that the coincidence between the burglary and the car theft is suspicious."

"So, you don't believe me?"

"The video of the suspect looks like you, and they have your license plate. What I really can't figure out, is why you were caught there. What is it you have against her?"

"Well, it's no secret that you're cheating with her, and you're married to my aunt."

"Wait a minute. Where did you hear that nonsense?"

"I didn't have to hear it. I saw it. At least on two occasions, I saw you visit her condo during late evening hours, when Aunt Erin was away teaching."

"So you're following me?"

"Why not? Someone needs to keep tabs on you for her sake."

"So that's it. You've appointed yourself her protector. What were you going to do to Suzanne?"

"I'm not admitting anything. But what I am saying is, you stay away from her, or I'll tell Aunt Erin all about you messing around with your boss, and you'll lose everything."

"So you're threatening me. What's this business with Irvine PD looking into you with regard to their body dump cases?"

"I don't know what you're talking about."

"They're working two homicide cases where attractive young ladies were dumped by a guy driving a Range Rover and were shot with a .25 caliber automatic. You have rented Range Rovers, and last time I checked, you own a .25 auto."

"Boy, now that's really conclusive evidence. That doesn't even sound like enough to get a search warrant. You've got a lot to lose, Uncle, the big house in Shady Canyon, the income Aunt Erin generates from that lucrative medical practice of hers, and the scandal of a romantic relationship with your boss could cost you those four gold stars on your collar. All I'm saying is you'd better put an end to that, and keep off my back, and everything will be cool."

"Get out of my office."

Chapter 55

The working environment within the Irvine Police Department's Communications Bureau had become increasingly tense over the days following Lieutenant Michael O'Brien's Mobile Data Computer transmission of a rumor that Scott Hunter and Dispatcher Valerie Mason had a sexual relationship. Knowing that it was false, her only recourse was to report her concerns to Internal Affairs. It was embarrassing, and she felt that it must be putting a strain on Hunter's relationship with his fiancée, Ashley Horton.

Lieutenant Paul Winthrop had interviewed both Mason and Hunter, who each denied having any romantic or sexual relations with each other, but made it quite clear that the rumor had never surfaced until O'Brien had transmitted it over the official electronic communications system. O'Brien had on many occasions been implicated in initiating gossip and rumors conveniently timed ahead of prospective promotions and transfers, but there had never been sufficient evidence to hold him accountable.

As with most investigations, criminal or internal, most of the potential evidence is collected prior to the interview of the accused suspect or employee. Lt. Winthrop had finished his data collection, and had given written notice for Lt. O'Brien to appear for an interview before Winthrop and his sergeant, and if requested, an attorney of his choice. O'Brien reported in uniform with his police officers' association attorney.

"Lt. O'Brien, my name is Lt. Winthrop, with the Irvine Police Department Internal Affairs Bureau. I have a few questions to ask you regarding an MDC (Mobile Data Computer) message that you sent to all terminals a few weeks ago. The message you sent stated, "reference my suspicions regarding the liaison between Hunter and Mason, I have it on good authority that it's a confirmed kill..." Is that correct?"

"That was a private textual conversation between Officer Ayers and me, and I have no idea how that could have been transmitted to all terminals."

"Were those words composed by you?"

"Well, yes, but they were simply intended for one person, and they were part of a larger humorous, fictitious story that was more fantasy than anything else. It was never presented as fact."

"Who was the good authority referred to in your text?"

"As I had indicated, it was a fantasy story to Ayers, in which I was wondering what it would sound like to have someone confirm that Lt. Hunter, who presents himself as a person of spotless character, was found to be a judgmental hypocrite."

"Do you not think that transmitting something of that nature over the system has a potential for causing harm?"

"I suppose so, but I never intended that to happen. I believe that the department is responsible for failing to upgrade the MDC system, as it has been reported often that such errors have been occurring."

"With that being the case, would you not consider it was ill advised to use the system for a message that could cause such a scandal?"

"It was a mistake, but certainly not malicious."

"Since you bring up the issue of maliciousness, was that not your intent to besmirch the character of Lt. Hunter to as many employees as possible?"

"Not at all. I had just had a congenial conversation with Lt. Hunter earlier that evening."

"Really? Had you not chided him for not solving two homicides actively under investigation, after he made a robbery arrest on the way in to work?"

"I never said such an outlandish statement. I simply told him that we missed him in Patrol."

"Isn't it true that you were critical of his investigative work, and recommended he come back to Patrol, and "play gunfighter with you?" "And, isn't it true that following your conversation with Lt. Hunter, you stayed hidden in the Detective Bureau, and heard a passing conversation between Lt. Hunter and Dispatcher Valerie Mason? Was it then that you came up with the idea of damaging Hunter's reputation when his discussion with Mason focused upon dispatchers missing his fiancée in the Communications Bureau, and when Mason asked you to say "hello" to his fiancée for her?"

"I did no such thing."

At this point, Lt. Winthrop produced Hunter's microcassette recorder and played portions of the recorded conversations between Hunter and O'Brien, and Hunter and Mason:

"Maybe if you would avoid these entanglements, you might solve a murder or two, and not have to stay late anymore. Or you could join me in Patrol and play gun fighter all you want."

"Good. How's Ashley? We sure miss her up in Dispatch."

"Sounds great. Please say hello for me."

At this point, O'Brien's attorney objected, on the grounds that Hunter had illegally recorded the conversations without O'Brien's consent. Winthrop responded:

"That's correct counselor, Lt. Hunter accidentally recorded the conversations, and was unaware that his recorder was on, until after his conversation with Mason concluded. Both Lt. Hunter and I are aware that in California, unless the conversation is related to a criminal offense, a private conversation cannot be recorded unless all parties agree to it. We are alleging that Lt.

213

O'Brien was engaged in the crime of slander against Lt. Hunter, and as such, the conversation would serve as evidence of that crime, in addition to the lies committed by Lt. O'Brien, which are admissible under the Brady decision. Brady holds that those lies would be discoverable in any legal proceeding in which Lt. O'Brien may testify, and could be used to impeach his testimony."

"Counselor, we are requesting that your client write a letter of apology to both parties slandered by his MDC violation, so that they can be posted on the Chief's bulletin board in the Patrol briefing room. I may also suggest you discuss with your client the advantages of retirement, since he is completely vested in the retirement system."

Chapter 56

It was one of those rare opportunities for a presidential visit during an election year. Even if the fundraising visit was not for the current President, former Presidents speaking on behalf of the Party warranted significant Secret Service protection, and much of that responsibility was supplemented by the local agency's Special Weapons and Tactics (SWAT) team. Hotels within the City of Irvine were frequent presidential destinations when campaigns selected Southern California venues for conservative events.

The protected party for this dignitary event was former President George W. Bush, who had visited Irvine during his presidency, as did his father, President George H.W. Bush, following the first Gulf War. Hunter was on the SWAT team for each of those events, and coordinated the security plan with the Secret Service during overnight stays at the Hyatt Regency Hotel.

Hunter walked the hotel grounds with the lead agent and placed SWAT officers in strategic locations in stairwells, on balconies, and at front and rear entrances. They would discuss scenarios for unusual occurrences, and develop options for addressing medical aid issues, trespass arrest protocols, and safe locations for evacuating a President if the hotel site could not be secured.

Based upon Hunter's previous experience, he was asked to assist in the Secret Service's command post located in one of the rooms in the hotel chosen for this particular visit, the Irvine Marriott. The Secret Service had requested a command officer from the local jurisdiction, capable of making decisions, and having the ability to summon additional resources if the circumstances warranted it. This would be a welcome break for Hunter, even though it was for only a one night stay.

Hunter recalled President George H.W. Bush's previous visit being particularly challenging. The President kept his watch on Washington, D.C. time to minimize jetlag, and he was an avid runner. Hunter was tasked with finding him a secluded running track that would require minimal additional staffing to cover the site. He found a private track owned by the Fluor Corporation, which was less than a mile away from the hotel. Still, the entourage included two limos, two Chevy Suburbans for the Counter Assault Team, one station wagon with a satellite dish, and two police patrol cars.

The speaking event was for a fundraising breakfast the following day. However, after the President's run, he discovered that a famous Mexican restaurant was located in nearby Costa Mesa. The Secret Service was sent scrambling to the site to conduct sweeps, and clear several portions of the restaurant to create safe zones large enough to accommodate the number of agents required to ensure that the President could complete a meal without curious onlookers interfering with his dinner. Despite some of the last minute challenging assignments, the Secret Service revered this President for the kind manner in which he and his wife, Barbara, treated them like family.

Hunter would be staying in the command post all night, so he expected that a former President would not generate much activity. He was overly optimistic, however. The visit had been posted in the Orange County Register, and it seemed as though all the crazies were coming out of hiding. Several calls of threats were forwarded to the command post, and agents were dispatched to numerous locations throughout Orange County. There were moments of quiet during the early morning hours, and Hunter was able to exchange stories with the agents, along with a Sheriff's sergeant assigned to the bomb squad.

"Hey Lieutenant, how'd you get interested in law enforcement?" An agent inquired of Hunter.

"When I was a kid, I would lie on the sofa with my Dad, and we would watch every episode of the TV series, "Dragnet." "I decided that I wanted to be like Detective Sergeant Joe Friday. He was played by the actor, Jack Webb, and he would always end the story with some catchy words of wisdom that would stick with you."

"How long did you have to work the jail before you got out on Patrol? A friend from Long Beach PD has a brother who is currently assigned to the jail with you guys." Hunter asked the Sheriff's bomb squad sergeant.

"What's his name?"

"The friend is the lead detective in Robbery/Homicide; his name is Bob Luther. His brother, Dave, has been a deputy with you guys for four years."

"Yeah, I remember him. He set some physical records at the academy. I think it was the obstacle course and push-ups. It takes about five years, and I hated most of it. It was difficult staying healthy with all the inmates who had poor hygiene, and the closed ventilation system. But once you got out on Patrol, you really knew how to spot an ex-con, and you knew how to talk to them to get the information that you needed. You could spot a scam very quickly."

"What was the craziest presidential protection story you can tell us?" Hunter asked the agents.

"I think it was the time we were protecting President Ronald Reagan at the United Nations in New York. Some of us assigned to the motorcade went to a "down room" for refreshments. I think it was Russian President Gorbachev's motorcade detail managed to sneak a bottle of Russian vodka into one of our limousines. We caught hell for that."

217

To cap off a long night, Hunter was invited by the Secret Service agent in charge to have a "photo-op," or photo opportunity with the former President. Hunter stood toward the end of a long line of dignitaries waiting outside a ballroom with huge black drapes shielding the photography stage for the "meet & great." He saw several movers and shakers of Orange County ahead of him, including one famous baseball coach. With Hunter towards the end of the line were the Captain of the California Highway Patrol Santa Ana station, and the County Sheriff. Hunter tried to think of something noteworthy to say to the President, but was having some difficulty being original.

When it was finally his turn, he was quite fatigued from staying awake all night. A presidential aide signaled for him to come forward and shake the President's hand. President Bush smiled and stated, "We sure appreciate all the work you folks have been doing for us."

Hunter replied, "Mr. President, our prayers are with you." The President smiled again and said, "Well, it's workin'."

Chapter 57

Tom Blackburn decided that he needed to meet with Bob Luther to see what comparisons could be made between their body dump case of Lena Holmquist, and Irvine's two pepper tree cases. He phoned Luther to confirm that he would be at work, and offered to take him to lunch after examining their evidence. He was hoping to develop enough probable cause to convince a judge to authorize a warrant to place a GPS tracker on Vannover's vehicle.

Luther met Blackburn at the front desk, and escorted him up to the Detective Bureau where a small conference room had been set aside for the Holmquist homicide, as had been done with Irvine's two cases. Blackburn read the interviews of Holmquist's husband, Alexander, the 322 Café's bartender, Guiseppi Scotto, Rusty Adderly, the sexual battery suspect, her friends, the Petersons, and the cab driver, the last person to see her alive.

At this point the only commonality with Vannover seemed to be the fact that he worked the evening that she was killed, got off work in time to have perpetrated the crime, and he had prior contact with the victim when she was battered by Adderly.

After Blackburn shared with Luther the report on the bloody shell casings they suspected belonged to Vannover and for which they were awaiting DNA results, he decided to also share some scuttlebutt he'd recently heard.

"One of my academy classmates is a burglary detective with Newport Beach PD. He told me that he got a case from Patrol in which your city manager's condo was burglarized in Newport Beach. The suspect vehicle was a pickup truck owned by

Vannover, but apparently Vannover had reported it stolen within an hour after the burglary was reported."

"Have they found his truck?"

"Not yet, but Newport I.A. (Internal Affairs) apparently notified your I.A. Bureau, and that's the last I've heard. My buddy was trying to interview Vannover, but was running into roadblocks from your station. He was either off duty, or was tied up on a call."

"Hey, I was just thinking. Why don't you contact your lab, and ask them to run those shell casings again for DNA. We might have run the DNA on our semen sample and .25 auto slug before your shell casings were tested. If that was the case, your shell casing blood might not show a hit. It would be great if the semen DNA matched the blood on your shell casings. Can you check to make sure your blood was compared to our semen sample and blood on our bullet slug?

"Sure, but we have to conclusively prove that it's Vannover's blood on the shell casings."

"Well, I was going to say, you should set up a surveillance on him and get some discarded DNA, but maybe we could get something discarded at our station like a soft drink, or a paper towel."

"Good idea. It's lunch time. Let's head down to Second Street to Domenico's. I'm buying."

Unfortunately, however Chief Steinhoffer was also leaving the station and saw Luther leaving with a detective whom the chief recognized from his Irvine days. Steinhoffer knew Tom Blackburn wasn't in the station just taking a tour. He was comparing notes on homicide cases. And Steinhoffer was angry.

~

Once again, Stephanie Winslow walked the ramp leading up to Turk's, armed with another piece of evidence – the photograph of Alex Vannover's swearing in ceremony at Long Beach PD.

Waitress Ginny Martinez couldn't make a positive identification from his academy photo, but maybe this picture would have a better result. When Ginny finished serving a couple in a nearby booth, Winslow withdrew the photo from her briefcase, placed it on the counter and asked the petite Hispanic waitress if anyone in the photo resembled the man she had served who had accompanied Kimberly Donahue.

"It sure looks similar to him, but I can't be sure."

"If you were to testify in a court of law, what percentage would you assign as to how sure you are that this was the man that you served the night that Kimberly Donahue was killed?"

"I'm so nervous, I think I would be 49-50% that this was who I served. He looks so different in a uniform."

"OK, thanks Ginny, we'll be in touch with you."

Chapter 58

The day of the annual Marine Corps / SWAT Team challenge march had arrived and Hunter was taking a break to participate. The Marine Corps Force Recon from Camp Pendleton would join Irvine's SWAT team in a march up Santiago Peak, the tallest point in Orange County's Saddleback Mountains, and upon reaching the summit they would helicopter down to their Tustin Helicopter Base for a barbeque.

The march is open to current and former members of the SWAT team, and the Marine Corps answer to the SEAL teams, "Force Recon," were all geared up and ready at the base of the mountain in Silverado Canyon. Silverado is an old mining town frozen in time with shack-like construction and vintage cafes.

Two Humvees filled with water were staged behind the two columns of tactical operators awaiting the command to march. The mountain was a mile high, but the dirt road leading to the summit stretched for twelve miles. Heavy rains the week before had cut deep cracks along the path from streams of water racing down the steep grade.

They began the ascent at 8:00 AM when the clouds were still overcast and the air was cool. Shortly after passing the first mile, the lead Humvee encountered a deep crevice across a path that measured approximately ten feet wide. The vehicle's right front wheel dipped into the jagged opening causing it to nearly flip off the edge of the mountain. The driver backed up and pressed forward at a different angle but achieved the same result.

It became apparent that the grade and the condition of the road had made passage impossible for the Humvees, so they backed down the mountain, leaving the teams with only the water in their canteens to last them the remaining eleven miles. The clouds were clearing and the intensity of the sun increased as the teams gained altitude.

Hunter stepped out from the lines and checked on the condition of the team members. It appeared that one of Irvine's snipers, Carl Evans, was encountering some distress. His face was flushed, but he didn't seem to be perspiring. Hunter determined that he was dehydrated, so he checked his canteen and found it empty. He gave him his canteen and asked if he wanted to continue. Evans was not one to be a quitter despite knowing that his condition was worsening, so he resumed the march.

At the five mile mark Evans began experiencing extreme lower back pain and the team medic's assessment was that he was passing a kidney stone. There was a clearing a few yards ahead where they moved him for a medivac to the hospital. Hunter hoped his cellphone could connect with a tower to summon a sheriff's department dispatcher. After walking further up the grade he hit four bars and spoke to the Sheriff's communication center. A Huey medical helicopter was dispatched from Fullerton airport, but was having difficulty locating the teams' position on the mountain.

A Recon ordinance technician activated a red smoke canister signaling their position and the Huey was hovering overhead. Evans was loaded onboard along with a team medic and the aircraft was off to Mission Trauma Center. No barbeque for Carl that day.

The teams pressed on as the California sun bathed the mountain with heat. To keep minds occupied, Marine sergeants began a series of Jodie calls, responsive marching rhymes, synchronized with the rhythm of their boots. A sense of unity and purpose bonded the teams with every step closer to the summit.

After passing the ten mile mark, Hunter received a phone call from Blackburn with an update following his lunch with Luther.

"I shared with Luther the information on his city manager's residence being burglarized, and the fact that Vannover's truck was seen leaving and later reported stolen," Blackburn stated.

"Had he been notified about the crime?"

"No, he hadn't"

"It doesn't surprise me. Steinhoffer's gonna try to keep a tight lid on something like that."

"Luther requested we run DNA on our shell casings again on the possibility that they had run the semen on their victim before we entered our shell casing DNA."

"Give it a try, and see if they can hurry things up a bit."

"Right, I'm sure that'll help expedite the processing. How's the march going?"

"Had to medivac Carl Evans to Mission. He got dehydrated and passed a kidney stone."

"Ouch! I thought you guys were bringing water."

"We did, but the road gave out, and the Humvees couldn't continue."

"Bummer. I hope Carl's all right."

"Yeah, hopefully we won't have any other surprises. This march is a gut-check. We hadn't counted on the weather being this hot. Call me if anything develops."

As the marchers wrapped around the southern side of the mountain, the panoramic expanse of the Newport coast and the Pacific Ocean came into view. Within the twenty-six mile swath of blue water separating Catalina Island from the coast were scores of tall masts and sun-bleached sheets of schooners, sloops, and ketches riding the wind.

The telecommunications equipment and antennas planted on the peak like needles in a pin cushion became visible from the final loop leading to the summit. Excitement became contagious as the end of the climb drew near. Hunter checked with a gunnery sergeant on the status of the two CH-53 helicopters assigned to take the twenty-five SWAT operators and thirty Marines to the Tustin air base. They would arrive in about twenty minutes.

Hunter looked to the west toward Bolero Peak, a mountain in the range slightly lower than the peak where he stood, and was surprised to see so many antennas arrayed across its summit. He turned to one of the SWAT sergeants and asked concerning their purpose.

"Sarge, do you know if any of the antennas there are associated with Orange County's telecommunications system for police and fire?"

"Yes sir, our repeater is on Bolero Peak. The ability for our patrol units to hear transmissions from fellow patrol units, instead of only dispatched calls is provided by the antenna on Bolero."

"How about those antennas over there? They look like cell towers."

"That's correct, sir. They're cell towers."

"Hmm, from this altitude the reception must be pretty clear."

Hunter thought for a moment, and then dialed Blackburn back on his cellphone.

"Tom, contact Vannover's cellphone carrier. We need to get a GPS history of his cellphone and crossmatch it with dates and locations related to each of the three homicide cases. I want to know if his cellphone was pinging cell towers near Suzanne Duncan's Newport Beach condo, Turk's restaurant, the Airporter Inn, the pepper tree, the Long Beach oilfield, and any other location you can think of. If his carrier gives you any static, start writing a search warrant. We've got plenty of probable cause now to convince even the most difficult of judges."

"I'm on it boss. I'll keep you posted."

The thundering turbines of the Marine Corps Super Stallion helicopters circled overhead as the SWAT / Recon teams assembled for boarding. Goggles were mandatory as dirt and rocks flew from the downdraft generated by the rotor blades. One copter would land, load, and depart, and then the next copter would follow the same procedure

The flight from the summit to the base was short. The huge blimp hangers could be clearly seen from the mountain top. The giant wooden structures now housed and maintained the CH-53 Super Stallions and CH-47 Chinooks, and were so mammoth that they created their own weather. Atmospheric conditions inside the Quonset-hut shaped buildings would occasionally create rain.

The flight from the mountain was windy, and the pilot banked some tight turns, but there were no complaints from the passengers, who were clearly entertained by the ride. Hunter and the teams devoured the barbequed carnitas and tortillas, and the beer flowed continuously from the kegs, but he couldn't stop thinking about the data he hoped would soon be provided to him from a suspect's cellphone.

Chapter 59

The call was dispatched as an active shooter or possible barricade at the 3700 block of Myrtle Avenue in Long Beach. The house was located on the corner of Myrtle and Bixby Road, across the street from Longfellow Elementary School. It was a single story home with brick and wood construction resembling French Tudor architecture. The resident, George Bishop, was a renter and army veteran who had suffered a brain injury from an Iraqi Improvised Explosive Device (IED).

Compounding Bishop's condition was the fact that he had Post Traumatic Stress Disorder (PTSD) flashbacks from time to time, and he threatened to commit suicide which resulted in two prior incidents requiring a police response. This Thursday, his neighbors reported that he walked out the front door armed with a World War II, M-1 Garand rifle, and fired several rounds into the air while screaming that "he couldn't take it anymore."

Good crisis negotiations had previously saved the day, but this morning's episode was the first time that firearms had been discharged. Dayshift patrol units quickly set up a perimeter, blocking off Olive Avenue, Bixby Road, Myrtle Avenue, and California Avenue. Longfellow Elementary School was evacuated to the north of the campus, with parents picking up children along Armando Road. Hughes Junior High School was also dismissed, with students evacuated to Roosevelt Road.

The command post was established on California Avenue in front of Hughes, which afforded the mobile command post vehicle land line phone communications, and additional restrooms. The Special Weapons and Tactics Team (SWAT) was activated, and was on-scene approximately 30 minutes following the initial 9-1-1 calls. Crisis negotiators were successful in convincing Bishop to answer the phone, and intermittent conversations were commenced with limited success in maintaining Bishop's attention.

Slowly, inner perimeter positions staffed by Patrol officers were replaced with SWAT operators, and high ground sniper positions were established on the roof of Longfellow Elementary, and in a second story bedroom in the house across the street, on the southwest corner of Myrtle Avenue and Bixby Road.

SWAT officer Ty Boyer was assigned by his team leader to load the armored BEAR (Ballistic Engineered Armored Response) vehicle with a sniper/observer team, and drive to a position on Bixby Road directly in front of Bishop's residence. Purchased through a Homeland Security grant, the BEAR is an armored vehicle with 800 lb. doors, a turret and gun ports, and is a larger, more ominous monster than its smaller brother, the Bear Cat.

Boyer's goal had always been to serve on a SWAT team, and for him, the added training for operating the BEAR was an exciting bonus. Both the Los Angeles Police Department SWAT and Los Angeles County Sheriff's SWAT teams had incidents involving law enforcement personnel from their departments who had been slain by barricaded suspects. The BEARS operated by those teams were instrumental in bringing their barricades to an end, when they successfully rammed and disassembled the structures concealing the suspects, revealing their positions for snipers.

Boyer's BEAR lumbered down Armando Road, turned left on Olive, and then left on Bixby. As he guided the armored monster into position in front of the barricaded house, Boyer witnessed a most peculiar event. Thoroughly intimidated by the tank facing his porch, Bishop exited the house with his hands in the air, and surrendered to the BEAR. A perimeter team of officers approached, and handcuffed Bishop before placing him in the backseat of a patrol car that was summoned to the scene. He was driven to the station, and subsequently transported to the hospital for a mental commitment.

Upon returning to the command post, Boyer was approached by a reporter and camera crew that was allowed access following the surrender. Although unprepared for an interview, Boyer gave a command performance in detailing the final moments that resulted in a safe conclusion to a dangerous situation.

"It was determined that we needed to tighten the containment of the suspect's residence, so we positioned our armored BEAR in front of his residence. Upon seeing the tank designed for urban rescue facing his front porch, he surrendered to the vehicle without incident..."

Boyer's soundbite was displayed on the evening news, which resulted in the activation of a long held tradition within the police culture. An officer, who is not regularly assigned as the department's press information officer (PIO), must provide ice cream for his shift, in the event that his interview is broadcasted on TV.

Chapter 60

This informal ice cream tradition would be anything but informal. But Luther would ensure that it appeared that way. They needed Vannover's DNA, and this was a perfect opportunity to procure it. The swing shift briefing for Long Beach PD would begin as normal with the sergeants reading the boards for wanted suspects and vehicles, and the daily 24 hour log would be reviewed. Detectives would sit in the back rows and offer tidbits on the cases they were working, and some would stand against the back wall, being available for questions from patrol officers.

Although the detectives were notorious for showing up at briefings to avail themselves of treats, this celebration would be orchestrated with precision. Officer Boyer's ice cream would be supplemented by some that was purchased by the Detective Bureau to make certain that everyone received a Haagen Das ice cream bar, or an ice cream sandwich. As always, soft drinks would be furnished, with equal numbers of regular and diet drinks in large plastic bottles, along with clear plastic disposable glasses, and a large package of napkins. A new addition to the refreshments would be dry roasted peanuts and cashews, poured into large bowls, to encourage the drinking of beverages.

Trash cans would be moved to the back of the briefing room, where detectives normally stayed, with designated detectives assigned to stand near each trash can, to identify and collect any item(s) touched by Vannover. Once Vannover discarded material, if he did not immediately leave the room, a detective would engage him in conversation, directing his attention away from the trash can into which he discarded his trash. Detectives retrieving Vannover's trash would appear to place their own trash into the basket, but would retrieve Vannover's, immediately leave the room, and head for the Detective Bureau.

The briefing began according to plan, with patrol sergeants made aware of the DNA operation, and encouraged to make their presentations short. Vannover entered the room with three other officers, and several others followed them in. He took a seat adjacent to the aisle, three rows in from the back. Detectives took their places in the back as planned, with the refreshments placed on the front table with the briefing boards and teletype sheets.

The boards were finished, and the floor was opened for questions. Few questions were asked, as officers were eager to get their ice cream before it melted. Officer Boyer gave a few words of appreciation for their support during the SWAT operation, and then the ice cream boxes were opened and drinks were poured. Vannover was seen selecting a Haagen Das bar, and poured himself a Diet Dr. Pepper. He finished his ice cream bar and grabbed a napkin before wiping his mouth. Prior to heading to the trash can, he put his wrappers on the table, and scooped a handful of peanuts with his right hand, while holding his drink in his left. He chatted briefly with an officer next to him, and then took a drink. Vannover picked up his wrappers and ice cream stick, and walked back to the trash can, where he dropped everything except the Dr. Pepper glass into the receptacle, and returned to his seat. He picked up his notebook with his right hand and put it under his left armpit, picked up his plastic glass, which was still half full of Diet Dr. Pepper, and walked out of the briefing room.

One detective had already retrieved Vannover's wrapper, napkin, and ice cream stick. A second detective followed him through the hall on his way back to the locker room to pick up his posse box, to take to his patrol car. Before entering the locker room, he took a final swig of his drink, and dropped the glass into a trash can in the hallway. Fortunately, the trash can was not close topped, and had been recently emptied, so the detective could identify the exact location of the plastic glass. All briefing room items with his DNA that had been discarded were retrieved and transported to the Detective Bureau, where they were packaged and hand carried by Luther to the crime lab for DNA analysis.

When he returned to his desk, Luther found a note taped to the receiver of his telephone: "From the desk of Chief Steinhoffer: Detective Luther, please see me when you return." Luther walked into his sergeant's office and presented the note to Sgt. Jason Horne.

"Sarge, do you know what this is about?"

"No, but I can guess. He must have seen us leaving for lunch with Tom Blackburn and recognized him."

Chapter 61

"Your note said that you wanted to see me, Chief?"

"Yes, Bob, I wanted to see you. Did I not tell you that I wanted to be informed whenever you have contact with Irvine PD regarding their homicide?"

"No, as I recall, you stated that before I <u>send</u> anything to Irvine, you wanted to be notified."

"That's not how I recall the conversation. What was Tom Blackburn doing in our station?"

"He wanted to compare notes on similarities between our homicide case, and his two homicide cases."

"When were you going to tell me about that exchange of information?"

"When we were finished exchanging information – today."

"You were clearly disobeying my directive to you."

"In what way?"

"You said that he wanted to compare notes. That sounds like he initiated the contact."

"He did."

"But I told you that I wanted everything cleared by me?"

"No, your original topic was regarding the sending of information. You did not make it clear that you wanted meetings cleared by you, just things being sent."

"You're playing games with my words."

"I am not. Surely you didn't mean that every step in a homicide investigation must be cleared by you. Nothing would ever get done. As I said, the purpose of your directive was related to my sending a photograph of a potential suspect in a homicide, which may involve both of our cities, and may involve your nephew."

"You're being insubordinate."

"I am not. But I do think you are obstructing a homicide investigation. And I think that I should have brought my sergeant in here with me as a witness. I know for a fact that both my sergeant and lieutenant have warned you about this very issue."

"That does it. You're suspended."

"On what grounds?"

"Insubordination. I gave you a directive, and you willfully disobeyed me."

"I just explained to you how any reasonable detective would interpret your directive. That's not insubordination. That's failure to be specific in your directions."

"I'm through discussing this issue. You're dismissed. Go home."

Prior to leaving the station, Luther responded to Sgt. Horne's office and explained the circumstances regarding his departure. Sgt. Horne then phoned Lieutenant Jerry Shaw, who was in a meeting with the deputy chief discussing the problem of interference by the chief of police. Luther then placed a call to Blackburn.

~

"Tom, this is Bob. The chief suspended me for insubordination."

"What? On what grounds?"

"He said that he had directed me to contact him whenever I had any communication with Irvine PD regarding their homicide cases. I told him that his direction was that anything sent to you guys, like the swear-in photo, had to be cleared by him. He disagreed, and suspended me."

"Well, how are they going to work your homicide?"

238

"We've got plenty of detectives, but you can go through my sergeant, Jason Horne. He's up to date on all the latest on both our cases."

"I'll share this with my boss, Lt. Hunter. He's not going to stand for this lack of cooperation between departments. As it stands right now, he thinks that your chief should have recused himself from all matters related to his nephew."

"Yeah, well the guy should not have been hired in the first place. By the way, did you happen to re-run your shell casings?"

"Funny you should ask. As we speak I'm driving to the court to get a judge to sign a search warrant for a tracker on our boy Vannover. The DNA came back from CODIS, and the DNA from the semen you collected from Holmquist matches the DNA on the bloody shell casings. Vannover is toast."

"Well, we collected his DNA from ice cream wrappers and plastic cups and we just received an analysis back from the crime lab, and Vannover's DNA is linked to all three homicides," Luther replied.

"Outstanding. He's been renting Range Rovers since he reported his pickup truck stolen. He's due to turn in his silver one tomorrow morning for a white one."

"How did you find that out?"

"The gal that rents him the Rovers has been keeping us posted on his rental activity. The white one he'll be renting already has a GPS tracker attached to it. I'm getting the warrant to make it legal when he picks it up. We don't want to let him slip away. We want to take him down in the morning."

"Wow, when you book him, we'll have him booked on the supplemental charges from our case."

"Sounds good."

Chapter 62

Following Luther's call to Blackburn, Hunter was briefed by Blackburn himself regarding Luther's suspension, and the interference being generated by Steinhoffer that was affecting both cases. Hunter immediately requested a meeting with Irvine PD's Chief of Police, Roger Chesterton.

Hunter entered Chief Chesterton's second floor office, which was on the corner of the civic center having the most expansive view of Barber Park and the Saddleback Mountains. His desk was teak with a matching wall unit adorned with trophies, police hats, plaques, and an official London Bobbie's helmet.

Chief Chesterton was in his mid-sixties, and his neatly parted hair was completely silver. He was tall, but thin and tanned by his frequent visits to the tennis courts. He was completely vested in the retirement system, and he was in his last year in law enforcement, which gave him considerable independence in making tough decisions. He was unintimidated by political correctness, and was encouraged by many to seek higher office. But this would be his final year, and retirement to a life with grandkids looked more appealing.

"Chief, I had mentioned to you in passing, that we had an unusual situation in the investigation of these pepper tree body dumps involving your predecessor's nephew. It has now come to a point in which your intervention may be warranted. During our investigation, we discovered that a person of interest in our two homicides, was also suspected in a Long Beach homicide. It's Long Beach Police Chief Daniel Steinhoffer's nephew, Alex Vannover. Vannover has been hired as a police officer with Long

Beach, after having served as a special deputy at the airport with the Orange County Sheriff's Department."

"We now have DNA confirmation that while working for the Sheriff's Department, Vannover committed our two homicides, and that while working in Long Beach, he committed a third murder in that city. Over the objections of his background investigator, Chief Steinhoffer hired his nephew. While detectives from our department shared information from our cases with the Long Beach detectives, they also provided information and evidence linking the three crimes.

Chief Steinhoffer has given a directive to the lead investigator in their case, Bob Luther, to clear any information with him before going to Irvine. When our own detective, Tom Blackburn, recently visited Long Beach PD to exchange information, Chief Steinhoffer suspended Detective Luther for insubordination. His rationale for this action is questionable, and has now made clearing these cases much more difficult. We have conclusive DNA evidence that Chief Steinhoffer's nephew is responsible for these murders, and these findings have been made possible through the cooperation of both Detective Bureaus, prior to Chief Steinhoffer's apparent interference on behalf of his nephew."

"My question to you, Chief," continued Hunter, "is there anything from your level that can be done to encourage Chief Steinhoffer to take the right course of action by restoring his detective. This would allow greater cooperation between our two agencies so that we can jointly prosecute these cases with the DA, and bring justice to the victims' families?"

"Hunter, from what you've just told me, I am also concerned Chief Steinhoffer may be completely compromised," replied Chesterton. "And that any overtures on my part, may be used against us when he communicates with his nephew. We have no idea about the dynamics of his family, or the relationships that may be motivating him to make these questionable decisions. You have enough evidence to make your arrest, and have sufficient information to add Long Beach's charges following Vannover's incarceration. I can certainly call Chief Steinhoffer and in a benevolent tone, ask that he consider re-instating his detective in an effort to assist us. But there are two possible outcomes. He could restore his detective to the case, or he could simply warn his nephew that we appear to be closing in."

"Whatever you feel would best facilitate your clearance of this case, I will support you. But, I can assure you, that based upon what you have shared with me, following Mr. Vannover's arrest on our cases, I will notify the State Attorney General's Office to investigate the Long Beach Police Department's handling of this matter, so that the fine reputation of those officers will not continue to be jeopardized by the unprofessional and possibly criminal conduct of their chief of police."

"Well Sir, I think that today and tomorrow are Vannover's days off, and that he could be anywhere. We've got a GPS tracker on a Rover he's supposed to pick up tomorrow. We're asking a judge to authorize a warrant for the tracker right now. We're also asking the judge for an arrest warrant, but we can still arrest him on sight, 836 PC (reasonable suspicion). We'll plan on taking him into custody at the car rental place tomorrow, and then you can call Steinhoffer to make your pitch. If for some reason we can't get him tomorrow, you can still make the call, Chief. It would sure be nice to have Long Beach at full strength, working with us to catch this guy. Heck, we may even take him into custody at work."

"So be it, Scott."

Chapter 63

Vannover had left word with Patti Nilsson at Paragon Executive Coaches that he would like to exchange Range Rovers around 10:00 AM. Blackburn had secured a search warrant signature from a judge, as well as an arrest warrant for California Penal Code Section 187, Murder. It was 9:00 AM, and a team of Irvine PD detectives had set up around the terminal at John Wayne Airport. Area 2 patrol officers had been advised of the new silver Range Rover the suspect was driving, and were warned that as a police officer, he was probably armed.

Hunter was on scene in his Crown Victoria, and thought that under normal circumstances they would need undercover vehicles to mask their intended take down of a murderer. However, since the location was the airport, there were frequently several marked police units at various locations within the terminal, so a few extra would draw little attention.

Patti Nilsson was understandably apprehensive about a possible arrest turning violent in her rental car lobby, so Hunter helped assuage her tension by assigning an attractive female officer dressed similarly to Nilsson behind the counter typing on a keyboard on a computer that was turned off.

The 10:00 hour came and went but there was no sign of Vannover. Hunter radioed to Blackburn:

"It's now 11:00 and it looks like he's not going to show. He's a murderer at large. It would have been nice to at least put a tracker on him."

"We have."

"What do you mean?"

"I put a GPS tracker on both of Paragon's Range Rovers. Now that we have the warrant, I'll just activate the other one."

"Hmm, well that's resourceful. Let me know when you have it up. I'm calling the Chief with an update."

~

"Hello, Chief Steinhoffer? This is Roger Chesterson, Chief of Police for the City of Irvine. How are you?"

"I'm fine, thank you. How are you getting along with that demanding bunch of ingrates of a city council I left you?"

"Well, they can be challenging, but I think I've figured out their motivations, and have learned how to keep them on the good side of the voters. The reason I'm calling this afternoon is to discuss those homicide cases our departments have been working so hard to solve. My understanding is that the detective that our people have been collaborating with on your department has been suspended."

Steinhoffer interrupted:

"Before we go any further with this, that suspension was a personnel decision that is a confidential matter. And quite frankly, I'm surprised, with all your experience, you would even bring it up."

"Please, Chief, hear me out. We are dealing with life and death issues that affect both of our cities. Ordinarily, I would never presume to interfere with something as sensitive as a suspension in a fellow colleague's organization. But in this case, I'm simply asking you to consider the totality of what we're facing with the brutal murders of innocent women. If you could find a way to reinstate Detective Bob Luther to assist us, we may have a better chance of saving lives. I can certainly appreciate the difficult position you are in, with your nephew being discussed as a person of interest."

"It is a weak case at best, and built entirely on coincidence. I don't see how one person can be so vital. There are many capable detectives who work these crimes. Surgeries, sickness, suspensions happen, and we adapt. I wish you luck in solving your cases. Good afternoon, Chief."

The phone connection ended. Chief Chesterson sent the following text message to Hunter:

"Scott, I spoke to Steinhoffer. Immovable on Luther suspension. Sorry I cannot report a better outcome. Please keep me posted on status of Vannover. Thx."

~

Chief Steinhoffer responded with his own text message – sent to his nephew:

"Alex, if you have an exit strategy for the many issues you are facing, I suggest you implement it. Irvine PD will soon be coming for you."

Chapter 64

Stephanie Winslow left Harbor Courthouse after having obtained the approval of her search warrant affidavits by the District Attorney's office, and a signature by a judge. She and a team of detectives headed to Costa Mesa to serve the warrant on Vannover's apartment, while several detectives at the airport waited for Blackburn's laptop to acquire the tracker on the silver Rover.

Upon arrival, they assembled in front of the management office, and received a key to the apartment unit. The apartment complex was a modern production by the Irvine Company, a quarter to a half mile west of the Crystal Court mall, a smaller shopping center directly behind the renowned South Coast Plaza.

The apartment buildings were two stories in height, with stand-alone units on each floor, and small backyards with built-in barbeques. The entire complex was surrounded by a tall wrought iron fence, painted green, with a sidewalk sitting atop a rolling greenbelt leading to the curb. To the rear was a sprawling carport with solar paneled roofs, and padlocked wooden storage boxes inside each parking stall. There was a large community pool, small gym, and clubhouse with billiard tables, kitchen, and large screen television for entertaining.

Vannover's unit was on the ground level near the pool. One of his three neighbors in the four-unit building had small bicycles, Big Wheels, and scooters on their porch, indicating children. However, it generally appeared to have residents who had not started families.

Winslow placed a call to Vannover's cell phone, but after four rings a recording played, and a prompt activated the voicemail.

She then knocked on the door and announced her name, agency, and search warrant information, while two detectives were posted by the back gate, in the event of an escape attempt.

Following no response, Winslow turned the key, and the three detectives with her entered, while two CSI techs waited by their van until notified the apartment was secure. After clearing the interior, which included two bedrooms, CSI was summoned to respond.

The scarcity of furniture and lack of picture frames gave a feeling of Spartan simplicity. The front room was Ikea with black leather sofa, rectangular pine coffee table painted black, two teak chairs, and a black and brown TV and storage unit against the wall. The kitchen eating area consisted of a circular butcher block table with dark brown legs, and two wooden chairs, with matching dark brown paint. The larger bedroom was filled with a king size bed, one black nightstand, and a matching, six-drawer dresser with an attached mirror. The bed was made with a gray blanket and white sheets, but no bedspread. The bedding, however, appeared almost military, with tightly pulled sheets and blanket, showing no signs of wrinkles or folds.

The spare bedroom had a bench press in the center, with a 145 lbs. barbell, and a set of dumbbells on the floor. In the far left corner of the room, propped against the wall, was a 6'2" light blue and white Dewey Weber surfboard. In the far right corner was a Yamaha acoustic guitar.

The closet in the larger bedroom contained clothes. However, the spare bedroom's closet was stacked with several boxes of 9mm, .25 caliber, and 12 gauge shotgun ammunition. Inside a .50 caliber ammunition can, were twelve magazines for a Glock 26 pistol, each filled to capacity with ten rounds of 9mm hollow point ammunition. No firearms were located within the apartment.

On top of the dresser in the bedroom was a rectangular-shaped men's jewelry dish, containing a brass uniform tie bar, one pair of gold cufflinks, and the 3-jeweled pendent necklace, described by Lena Holmquist's husband, along with several women's pierced earrings and various keys. The jewelry and ammunition were photographed in place, and then seized as evidence. Photos were then taken of the entire interior of the apartment, and documents were found that the detectives thought might help in finding Vannover, and locating and additional places where evidence could be secreted, such as storage lockers.

~

The evening had rapidly arrived, and a new development also arose during the search warrant service at Vannover's apartment. Costa Mesa Police discovered his pickup truck in the Macy's parking lot at South Coast Plaza. Fortunately, Winslow had included the Chevy Silverado in the "areas to be searched" box of the warrant, so the vehicle could be immediately processed by CSI. After clearing the apartment, Irvine detectives and CSI technicians responded to the Macy's parking lot and met with Costa Mesa patrol officers standing by the pickup truck.

Winslow had found a spare key to the Silverado on Vannover's dresser and opened the door for CSI processing. She expected that they would find additional DNA evidence linking it to the Holmquist murder.

251

Chapter 65

The next morning, Hunter was really becoming concerned that Vannover's case could become a repeat of a former Los Angeles Police officer who killed an Irvine couple before going on a rampage through Southern California, leaving dead police officers along his path of escape. He had worked that case, and wasn't looking forward to the possibility that Vannover would follow his example.

Blackburn had now gotten the GPS running on the silver Range Rover; and the coordinates showed that the vehicle was in the northern area of Orange County near Silverado Canyon. This little village at the base of Santiago Peak was a page out of the Wild West and the mining culture brought about by the gold and silver rush. The mountains and canyons around Silverado were sites where Orange County's earliest lawmen had shootouts with robbers and desperados. Hunter couldn't help wondering if Vannover's motives for being in the area had some connection to those long-ago crimes or if he might simply be trying to create a timeline for a departure from the state, or even the country.

While pondering these possible connections, Hunter received a text from Winslow that Vannover's apartment and truck had been searched, and that his former roommate had been located at his place of employment in Corona. She stated that according to his roommate, they had surfed Rosarita Beach in Mexico, and that Vannover was familiar with the towns south of the Mexican border. She also said that he owned two surfboards, that one was missing from his apartment, and that he was probably in possession of a Glock 9mm pistol, Beretta .25 caliber pistol, and a Remington 12-gauge shotgun.

Blackburn radioed that the GPS signal he was receiving was intermittent due to the mountainous terrain. But within 20 minutes, Blackburn reported that his laptop had reacquired the signal, and was tracking the Rover in the city of Yorba Linda. Yorba Linda, home of the Nixon presidential library, was a small city patrolled by the Orange County Sheriff's Department.

Upon discovering Vannover's new location, Hunter phoned Sgt. Keith Miller at the station and requested that he make certain that the suspect's murder warrant had been entered into the Wanted Persons System, and asked that he have Dispatch notify the Sheriff's Department that he was currently driving through their contract city. Sgt. Miller then provided a very important update.

"Lieutenant, I was able to obtain Vannover's phone records. The closest cell tower to Old Barranca Road was located near the Irvine Unified School District's administrative offices. So far, on the dates and approximate times of our two homicides, Vannover's cellphone "pinged" the tower by the school district. He was definitely in the area of that pepper tree. I'm now working on cell towers in Long Beach, then Turk's."

"Good work, Keith. Please keep me posted."

~

At 9:00 a.m., Vannover entered the Dick's Sporting Goods on Savi Ranch Parkway to purchase an extra sleeping bag and camping blankets for his destination along Rosarita Beach in Mexico. He figured that every peace officer between Los Angeles and Orange Counties would be looking for him, based upon his uncle's cryptic text.

He hoped he would have time to lay low under the cops' radar long enough to start a new life south of the border. After checking out at the sporting goods store, however, he saw an Orange County Sheriff's deputy in the parking lot. While it would turn out that the deputy was only there to purchase fresh batteries

254

for his flashlight, Vannover refrained from making eye contact, since he was sure the deputy was trying to confirm facial recognition. Panicking, he dropped his bags of camping supplies to the ground, drew his 9mm Glock, and fired three rounds in rapid succession, striking the front panel of the deputy's body armor, and his left bicep.

Although injured, the deputy fell back into a parked car while drawing his Sig Sauer 9mm and was able to return fire in Vannover's direction. The uninjured Vannover raced toward the Range Rover, jumped into the driver's side door, and turned on the ignition. The deputy fired two more rounds, striking the rear window of the Rover, but they impacted at such an oblique angle, they glanced off without penetrating. Vannover roared out of the parking lot, as the deputy radioed "998," officer involved in gun battle.

Chapter 66

Within minutes, Hunter heard the countywide "Red Channel" broadcast of a deputy involved in a gun battle in Yorba Linda with a suspect driving the silver Range Rover they were currently tracking. His worst fears had begun to materialize.

Vannover knew that a countywide broadcast would be forthcoming, and that shortly thereafter, freeway checkpoints throughout Orange County would be staffed, so he remained on surface streets. He felt the tension rise as he realized his chances of survival were rapidly diminishing.

As the Range Rover approached Angel Stadium, an Anaheim Police motor unit spotted Vannover and radioed for assistance. Units from both cities converged on the location as Vannover realized he'd been found. He entered the Katella on-ramp to the 57 Freeway and sped south toward Interstate 5, with Anaheim and Orange units in hot pursuit.

At this point, an Anaheim motor officer radioed a request for air support from his station. His Dispatch Center reported that their helicopter "Angel 1" was down for repairs. Immediately Anaheim Dispatch requested the Orange County Sheriff's Department to assist with their helicopter, but was told that "Duke 1" was refueling at John Wayne Airport.

With no air support available, the pursuit continued to the Jamboree Road off ramp in Irvine, where Vannover veered onto the exit heading southbound. Now the Irvine units could pick up the pursuit, as Orange and Anaheim units disengaged. Vannover continued, swerving down Jamboree Road past the 405 Freeway, where Hunter and the detective units were trailing the marked police cars as they approached the City of Newport Beach.

Now Hunter and Blackburn joined the chase in Hunter's staff car, with Blackburn sitting in the passenger seat, following the pursuit electronically with his laptop. They crossed Campus Drive into Newport Beach, and approached the fork at Jamboree and MacArthur Boulevard. Vannover remained on Jamboree Road, and as he approached San Joaquin Hills Drive, a Newport Beach Police officer who had just left his station, deployed spike strips at San Joaquin Hills. The right side tires of the Rover deflated, but Vannover continued southbound on his flattening tires.

As Vannover grew closer to the residential areas where Suzanne Duncan lived, he roared down the neighborhood streets with which he was now familiar, and lost the marked patrol units. Blackburn's laptop also lost the signal, so Hunter stopped and waited near Bayside Drive.

Suddenly, Blackburn reacquired the signal, and Hunter sighted the Rover driving southbound on Marine Avenue, and resumed the chase onto Balboa Island. Hunter now realized that Vannover had only two avenues of escape – back the way he entered the tiny island, or riding the ferry across the channel to the Balboa Peninsula. There were only five streets on the island surrounded by magnificent estates, with expansive water views. Although the Range Rover would normally not stand out in this neighborhood, the shreds of the tires blown by the spikes strips had severely battered the sheet metal of the Rover making it easy to identify.

Vannover turned right on Park Avenue heading toward the Balboa Ferry. It was a dead end street terminating at the water. The ferry could easily be seen traveling midway across the channel.

His heart pounding, Hunter pulled directly behind the Rover, put his Crown Vic in "Park," opened his driver's door, and drew his .45 caliber Sig Sauer pistol. He aligned his front and rear sights on Vannover, who was still seated, and holding the steering wheel. Blackburn followed Hunter's firearm procedures from the passenger side, with his 9mm Smith & Wesson M & P pistol.

Vannover suddenly opened his door, and stood facing Hunter while pointing his Glock 26. Vannover started pulling the trigger as fast as the joints in his finger could move. Blackburn returned fire. His first round missed, but the second round struck Vannover's right leg, apparently severing the femoral artery. Hunter double tapped, with the first round striking Vannover's left hand, and the second round entering his chest, below the left clavicle. Supporting his pistol, Blackurn put his third round into Vannover's right shoulder, blowing out his rotator cuff. Vannover spun clockwise, falling across the driver's seat, striking the gearshift lever with his elbow, and throwing the transmission into "Drive."

The Range Rover rolled off the pier, into the water, and began to sink into the channel. The open driver's door pinned Vannover's legs against the door frame, as water pressure pinched tighter with the increasing depth. In those remaining seconds of consciousness, Vannover's blood pressure plummeted from blood loss, making him barely lucid. However, he was still aware that the Rover had filled with water, and that he was too weak to break free. His worst fear had become reality – dying in deep water.

Hunter and Blackburn looked toward each other across the front seat of the Crown Vic:

"You OK?"

"Yeah."

"You hit?"

"No."

Thumbs up.

Chapter 67

It took nearly an hour for a heavy tow and dive team to arrive and lift the Rover from the channel. Sergeant Miller came soon after, along with Detective Winslow, who removed the weapons and ammo from the car, and took possession of Vannover's cellphone. The coroner took custody of Vannover's body, wallet, and badge case, and the District Attorney's shooting team brought twelve investigators to the scene to assist in the investigation.

Hunter assigned two detectives to work with the D.A. team, while he and Blackburn returned to the station, where a psychologist met them for debriefing. Following his required psychological exam, Hunter called the Sheriff's Department to check on the status of the wounded deputy. Fortunately, his surgeons successfully reattached his wounded left bicep, and the prognosis was good for restoration of the full use of his arm.

Hunter began to second guess his decision to ask Chesterton to contact Steinhoffer on behalf of Luther. Luther's help on the case had been instrumental in making the bloodwork fall into place, and he was seen as a tremendous resource for clearing all three homicides, and possibly more. But, it seemed as though the case sped in the wrong direction the moment an overture was made to Steinhoffer.

Hunter returned to his office to begin writing his supplemental report, beginning with the judge's signature on Blackburn's GPS search warrant. He would hold off writing the pursuit and gun battle until a few days had passed, so that his mind could properly organize the chronology of events.

After typing the first two paragraphs, he stopped to see who was standing in his open doorway. Miller stood holding

Vannover's cellphone, now dry, after he had borrowed a hairdryer from CSI.

"Hi Scott, nice work on that pursuit and takedown of Vannover today. Glad nobody got hurt. But I've found something pretty incredible on his phone. There's a text message from Steinhoffer."

Miller handed Hunter the phone:

"Alex, if you have an exit strategy for the many issues you are facing, I suggest you implement it. Irvine PD will soon be coming for you."

"Wow Keith. I'm not surprised, but it's kind of interesting that he would put this in writing. I would bet that he couldn't reach him on the phone to tell him so he elected to text him because he's family. It certainly explains why we suddenly couldn't find him, and the timing of the text leaves no doubt as to what made him flee."

"Yeah, the way I see it, these statements clearly make a case incriminating Steinhoffer as an accessory after the fact to murder."

"They may file it that way Keith, but the three-piece suits will bargain it down to something else."

"The shrink put you off for a few days?"

"Yep, and Ashley and I will be putting that time to good use. Come on, we need to meet with the chief about this phone message. He'll want to move pretty quickly on this."

~

Chief Chesterton greeted Hunter, Miller, and now Blackburn and Winslow who had joined the group in the Chief's office, praising them for the great work they had accomplished in taking down a serial killer. The press had gathered in the piazza area at the station entrance waiting for a press conference. However, Chesterton wanted to keep the names of the shooting officers confidential until they had finished their decompression period. Now, he wanted to ensure that they were properly praised for the difficult job they had performed under some challenging dynamics.

"This case certainly involved a broad spectrum of tactics to solve. You all have done a great job in putting it together and capturing an extremely dangerous suspect."

"Thanks very much, Chief. But we also wanted to show you this message on the suspect's cellphone that will give you some insight as to why this murderer was so difficult to identify and capture," Hunter replied.

Hunter motioned for Miller to pull the message up for the Chief. Chesterton read the two sentences, and continued to stare at the screen, thinking carefully in choosing his words.

"This is a sad day in many ways. Vicious murders were committed by one of our own, but the leader of one of California's largest police departments violated his oath of office in protecting that individual."

"It explains why we were running into so many roadblocks, Chief," Hunter responded.

"Well, I had made it clear to him that his suspension of the lead investigator on the case his agency was handling was jeopardizing ours, but he refused to listen. Now with his text, he has left me no alternative but to contact the Attorney General and request his department investigate Chief Steinhoffer."

Chapter 68

It didn't take long for the press to converge on the Long Beach Police station when the serial killer was identified as an officer with their department. Within hours, they had discovered that the officer was the nephew of the chief of police, and Steinhoffer was summoned into Duncan's office for damage control.

"Why on earth did you hire him in the first place? The rumors are out that he was trouble with the Sheriff's Department?"

"We had no indication of any criminality, just some maturity challenges."

"Criminality? Your punk nephew was chasing women before we even hired him. The Sheriff's had it well documented."

"Two anonymous calls alleging he asked women for dates, does not seem sufficiently credible to disqualify a candidate."

"Then you fail to take action when he breaks into my condo? I was going to be his fourth victim. Or who knows, maybe there are even more victims out there."

"First it was your ridiculous venture with the spike strips, and now you've brought this ticking time bomb of a nephew within our midst. I'm going to have to suspend you and put your deputy chief in charge. Then I'm going to test the political winds with the Council to see if I have enough votes to support my firing of you. You're at will, I can legally do it, but I'm going to make sure my back's covered on this one."

"You're really planning to do that? I would be very careful. I might just have to file a sexual harassment charge against you," Steinhoffer replied.

"Harassment? You were the one who was chasing me," Duncan shot back.

"You have to remember Suzanne, you're my boss, and I'm the subordinate. The organizational relationship puts you in the superior position, and I'm placed at a disadvantage to your position of strength. This could be viewed as a Quid Pro Quo. Don't forget, I'm an attorney."

"Boy, you're playing some high stakes poker. With your reputation, and your authoritative position as a police chief, I'll take my chances. You may go now. I'll have your secretary request your deputy chief to meet with me now."

~

The following morning, the Attorney General for the State of California notified the media that a 3:00 PM news conference would be scheduled regarding an investigation related to the alleged improprieties within the Long Beach Police Department. Timed to correspond with the network evening news, the news conference would focus on alleged actions taken by the former chief of police in obstructing the investigation of several murders within the Los Angeles and Orange County areas.

~

"Good afternoon, ladies and gentlemen. Recently, the Attorney General's office received credible information that former Long Beach Police Chief Daniel Steinhoffer allegedly aided and abetted his nephew, former Long Beach Police Officer Alex Vannover, in avoiding apprehension for the murders of Kimberly Donahue, Wendy Gilbert, and Lena Holmquist. Investigators from the Attorney General's office will be launching an investigation into these charges, as well as other charges alleging that he obstructed the investigation of these murders, and possibly the investigation into the residential burglary of a Long Beach city official."

"The Donahue and Gilbert homicides, investigated by the Irvine Police Department, and the Holmquist homicide, investigated by the Long Beach Police Department are believed to

266

have been perpetrated by Chief Steinhoffer's nephew. Investigators believe that the Donahue and Gilbert murders were committed during the time that Mr. Vannover was employed by the Orange County Sheriff's Department as a special deputy, assigned to the John Wayne Airport. The Holmquist murder was alleged to have been committed while he was employed by the Long Beach Police Department. Anyone having information regarding any of these crimes is encouraged to contact the agencies whose numbers are posted on your screen."

Chapter 69

They had planned this trip for months; but chose to tie it into the mandatory 7-day paid time off to decompress from the officer involved shooting. Since Scott and Ashley had been Disneyland annual pass holders for several years, they elected to discover what Hawaii would be like if the adventure was Disney-themed.

Flying to the island of Oahu, they landed on Honolulu, and then traveled by bus to the far end of the island where Disney had created the Aulani resort on a Hawaiian beach. In the Disney tradition, the hotel was built around an artificial Matterhorn-like mountain with water slides. Circling around the mountain were river rapids, pools, fountains, and scavenger hunts based upon Disney movies. Some restaurants were inhabited by Disney characters, and some were perched overlooking a private beach, surrounding a romantic lagoon.

They arrived before dusk, and watched the sunset, eating sushi while sipping Mai-Tai's. All of the employees were "cast members," meant to give guests the sensation of participating in a play or a movie, ensuring that their visit was "magical."

Their room faced the ocean with a white sand beach, and a lagoon shaped similarly to the Neverland destination in Peter Pan. Above the beach, were acres of manicured green grass, flowers, and tropical vegetation divided by a sidewalk leading to adjacent resorts. The teak furniture and Pacific island décor gave the impression of a ship's cabin that was almost seaworthy.

Too tired the first day from hours of travel, they hit the pillows early by west coast time. But the three hour time difference required adjustment. Their second day began with coffee, brought to the room by Scott, but harvested from a hillside in Kona. A morning jog along the beach worked up an appetite for a hearty breakfast at the beachfront restaurant serving eggs, sausage, and the island favorite: POG – pineapple, orange, and guava juice. The uniforms for the day: shorts, Hawaiian shirt, sun dress, and sandals.

A day of snorkeling took Scott and Ashley to a beach with black rock cliffs and crystal clear waters teaming with multi-colored fish, turtles, and an occasional visiting porpoise. Following the evening meal of wine, Mahi-Mahi, and macadamia nut pie, a walk across the street took them to a mall of tiny shops with Hawaiian shirts, tropical jewelry, oil paintings, and scrimshaw.

Back in their room, wine in hand they watched the evening lights of dinner cruises, sailboats, and occasional ocean liners. Ashley quietly retreated to the bathroom, and emerged after changing into a costume she had hidden in her suitcase.

Scott turned around. Standing in the doorway was Ashley clad in a Minnie Mouse red baby-doll with white polka dots, black mouse ears, red with white polka dot hair-bow, spiked high heels, and a hint of Shalimar perfume.

Scott was speechless.

Chapter 70

For several weeks, Hunter, Blackburn, Winslow, and Miller wrote investigative supplemental reports to the initial crime reports of the murders of Kimberly Donahue and Wendy Gilbert. Each piece of evidence was carefully documented, and woven into the tapestry of the homicide investigations. Hunter had taken copious notes to ensure that all of the interviews were followed up, and made certain he read every report written by his detectives, so that there were no discrepancies or contradictions.

The Long Beach Police Department's deputy chief had been elevated to acting chief, and had reinstated Detective Luther, so that he could coordinate with Irvine detectives and build his case for clearance. His first order of business, following the completion of the homicide case, was to prepare a report detailing every step in the Holmquist case in which he was obstructed or delayed by Steinhoffer, and every conversation with him regarding the hiring of his nephew.

Hunter prepared an outline of the chronological events leading to Vannover's shooting, which he would eventually use in writing his account for the murder case. It would also be used as a guide for his interview with the district attorney's investigators working the shooting report. Because it normally takes 5-6 months for the completion of an "officer involved shooting report," Hunter expected he would be the last person to be interviewed. The only criteria upon which they would base their findings were whether the shooting officer reasonably feared for his life.

Hunter and Blackburn scheduled a lunch with Luther to congratulate his return to the Detective Bureau. After their meal they went to the nearby oilfield crime scene where Lena Holmquist had been dumped by Vannover, then headed back to the Long Beach Police station using the probable route her killer had taken.

After dropping Luther off at his station, Hunter received a call from Winslow requesting they meet her at Steinhoffer's next door neighbor's house in Shady Canyon. Jim and Sally Prescott, Steinhoffer's neighbor, had found a strange recording on their home's closed circuit video system.

Sally told the officers that Jim had been reviewing and changing the video disks to their system because he remembered that several months ago, Erin O'Connell, Chief Steinhoffer's wife, had complained to them about the vandalism that was occurring on their street, which she and Jim had attributed to some of their teenage daughter's friends.

"We were having mailboxes blown up by cherry bombs, and houses being toilet papered," said Sally, "and Dr. O'Connell had complained that these kids were waking her up at night, and were making her tired for surgeries she was performing the next day. As a result of her complaints, we bought this video system with cameras installed around the exterior of our house, and picked up this strange video on our machine."

The recording clearly showed a silver Range Rover slowly passing in front of the house during nighttime hours. A few seconds later, a man's figure resembling Vannover's build was seen walking past the front of the house, and disappearing along the side of the house adjoining Steinhoffer's yard.

Then, a Ford Escape displaying the logo for the private security company patrolling the gated community, slowly passed by. Next, the male subject was seen running in front of the Prescott house in the direction from which he came.

Jim added, "We saw on the news that silver Range Rover belonging to Chief Steinhoffer's nephew being fished out of the

272

ocean and thought maybe this tape would help your investigation.

"I'm going to take a look over there, just to check it out," Winslow said.

Walking out the front door and down the herringbone brick steps leading to the sidewalk, she looked up at the massive two story white colonial house with the carriage driveway looping in a "U" shape past the tall, circular pillars. As she walked up the steep mound of grass separating the two homes, she made a quick glance under the eaves of the Prescott's roof, and found the camera that had captured the scene she had just viewed.

Standing between the two homes, Winslow first examined the shrubbery in the planter along the south wall of the Prescott house, which ended at the six foot block wall shielding the backyard. She checked each window for pry-marks, and the screens for punctures or bent metal, but found everything intact.

She then turned and faced the Steinhoffer/O'Connell residence and repeated the procedure on their side of the property. The landscaping along the north wall of their single story ranch house consisted of large hibiscus bushes with an ivy ground cover. Between two hibiscus bushes was a natural gas meter, with the ivy ground cover matted down flat, with the leaves and stems broken, as if crushed under foot by a meter reader. However, upon closer examination, Winslow discovered a small blasting cap, with two wires extending out through the bottom. From her training, she recognized these devices as initiators for exploding dynamite, and backed away, while retrieving her cellphone. She knew the approximately inch long metal cylinder with electrical wires extending out the bottom resembled an oversized transistor, but it could pack a powerful punch.

"Hey Boss, I found a blasting cap next to Steinhoffer's gas meter. You better come check it out."

273

"Is it attached to anything?" Hunter asked.

"No, there's no dynamite or high explosives. It looks like it just fell here. But we better call the bomb squad to collect it; if these things aren't handled right they can blow your hand right off."

Hunter and Blackburn met with Winslow, while the Prescott's waited on the sidewalk.

"What do you think, Lieutenant?" Winslow asked.

"He could have been setting up a bomb for either Steinhoffer or his wife, or both, and the security vehicle frightened him off. Go ahead and call Dispatch, and have them contact the Sheriff's Department, and get the bomb squad out here. Tom, can you take a picture of this with your cellphone camera?"

Hunter walked next door to the Steinhoffer residence to see if anyone was home. He rang the doorbell, with no response. He dialed the chief's cellphone number he had in his directory from the time that he worked for him, and found that he hadn't changed his number. But the call went immediately to voice mail.

Hunter then looked up the number for Dr. Erin O'Connell's medical practice, and was connected with her receptionist. He left a message for her to call, but left no details, other than it was regarding her house.

"Lieutenant Hunter, please."

"Speaking."

"Lieutenant, this is Dr. Erin O'Connell returning your call. Is there something wrong with my house?"

"Doctor, your neighbors, the Prescott's, have a video camera system they installed to address the vandalisms in your neighborhood, and discovered that your nephew had possibly dropped something next to your home several evenings ago. After we checked the side of your house where your gas meter is located, we found a blasting cap that's used to ignite dynamite. By itself, it's like a giant firecracker, but attached to a high explosive, it initiates a larger blast. We have the bomb squad on the way to collect it, we don't want anyone getting hurt picking it up. Would you have any idea why your nephew might leave or have dropped something like that?"

Hunter suddenly realized that he should have had Winslow place this call, but didn't believe that his name had been released yet as one of the shooting officers of the doctor's nephew.

"Lieutenant, I'm so devastated by the events that have impacted our family. I can't possibly fathom why Alex would do any of the things he has been accused of. Could that device you mentioned have been placed there by one of the kids that have been savaging this neighborhood?"

"I don't think so. Blasting caps are something that adults would be dealing with. I understand you're upset, and it is a difficult time for you. I've tried to reach Chief Steinhoffer, but his phone went immediately to voice mail."

"Well, we're separated now, and our Irvine house has been listed for sale. I moved out some time ago to Newport, and Daniel recently moved somewhere in Irvine. I'm sure if you leave him a message, he'll get back to you."

"Thanks doctor for calling me back. We should have this cleared from your property shortly. If anything comes to mind, or if you should have any questions, please feel free to contact Detective Stephanie Winslow at the number I will be texting you."

Hunter briefed Blackburn and Winslow on his conversation with Dr. O'Connell, and told Winslow she would be the doctor's point of contact, since he and Blackburn were the shooting officers. As the bomb squad's truck arrived on scene, Blackburn shared his information about the discovery of the explosive device.

"Lieutenant, I've been thinking about a rumor that Luther shared with me about Steinhoffer. He said that several detectives and some command staff believed that Steinhoffer and City

Manager Suzanne Duncan had an on/off romantic relationship. Vannover's nephew status to Steinhoffer was by marriage. Maybe Vannover found out about the romance rumor. The guy seems crazy enough to want to "off" his adulterous uncle for cheating on his aunt."

"Well, right now we can only guess," Hunter replied.

Chapter 71

The Attorney General's investigation culminated in the indictment of Chief Daniel Steinhoffer for accessory after the fact to murder. Whether the chief's attorneys would successfully plea bargain the charges down to obstruction of justice remained to be seen. However, for now, the chief had pleaded not guilty.

Adding to the insult of the indictment, he was booked in his own jail, and then released on $1million bail. His attorneys successfully argued that Los Angeles County would be a prejudicial environment for his trial to take place, so the venue was changed to Orange County.

Steinhoffer was directed to have a supplemental booking into Orange County Jail. The dayshift booking deputy was Dave Luther, Detective Bob Luther's brother. The former chief was fortunate that his encounter with Luther's brother wasn't in jail housing. Since he was posting bail, he would not have to live with Dave Luther as his module deputy.

"Well, good afternoon, Chief. Will you be staying with us? Oh, I see that you will be bailing out. Do you know who I am?"

"Not really."

"My nametag says, "D. Luther," as in Dave Luther, brother of Detective Bob Luther, Long Beach PD."

"Oh."

"Did you hear that he's been reinstated by the new chief?"

"No."

"Yes, justice has been done. Hopefully justice will be served in your case as well."

Former Chief Steinhoffer completed the booking process in the normal three hours, and was then released on bail. Following the separation from his wife, his temporary home became an apartment in the Spectrum district in Irvine.

~

Steinhoffer's trial lasted three weeks, with Hunter, Blackburn, and Luther all subpoenaed to testify. The critical piece of evidence was the text message he sent to his nephew, following the call from Irvine's Chief Roger Chesterton requesting that he reinstate the lead investigator on Long Beach PD's murder case, Detective Bob Luther.

The timeline established by Hunter showing the time of Chesterton's phone call, the GPS coordinates showing Vannover in Silverado Canyon, the time of the attempted murder of the sheriff's deputy, and the time when the pursuit was initiated, were all damning evidence.

Over his attorneys' admonitions, Steinhoffer elected to testify in his own defense. Under cross examination, the deputy district attorney boxed him in by arguing that he texted his nephew to put an "exit plan" in motion. This statement, coupled with "Irvine PD is coming soon," weighed heavily in the reactions on the faces of the jurors. It was apparent that the defendant was, in fact, suggesting his nephew should flee.

Attorneys for Steinhoffer recommended they negotiate a plea bargain to a lesser charge of obstruction of justice, to which the former chief vehemently objected. However, Luther's testimony regarding his suspension, and his initial recommendation that Vannover not be hired were so compelling that Steinhoffer's lead attorney threatened to quit.

Steinhoffer pled guilty to felony obstruction of justice, but was sentenced to one year in jail, followed by probation, which if violated, would result in prison. He was directed to serve his sentence in the Huntington Beach city jail.

Chapter 72

The Dojo humidity was so thick that the Shihan's (chief instructor) glasses fogged, and the bank of mirrors along the west wall dripped with condensation. Spring nights were frequently humid from the rain, but the evenings' advanced karate classes generated tremendous heat from the half hour warm-ups.

Hunter's rank was Godan, fifth degree black belt, technically qualifying him for the title of sensei, but his chief instructor's rank was eighth degree, so he joined the other high ranking black belts in the front row to set the example for the class in following the Shihan's instruction. Hunter was fortunate to have a direct link to the Orient from his chief instructor, who was one of the few Caucasian Americans who had received his rank in Japan from Tokugawa, the great-great-great grandson of the 15th and final Shogun (warlord) from the island famous for its heritage in the martial arts.

Basics and kata (form exercises) comprised the warm-up, but since it was the second Tuesday of the month, the instruction would consist of ju-jutsu based self-defense. This evening's technique involved a carotid restraint, which fit nicely into the curriculum Hunter taught as one of five defensive tactics instructors for the police department.

The carotid restraint was frequently confused with a "choke" hold. It involves forearm and bicep pressure applied on the assailant's carotid arteries on both sides of the neck. The flow of blood to the brain is restricted, causing unconsciousness within seconds. However, through improper training many officers applied pressure to the throat, restricting oxygen and frequently causing injury to the windpipe. Other injuries or death resulted from applying the carotid too long and causing brain damage. The technique was extremely useful in controlling violent individuals, but it required extensive training to achieve successful outcomes.

The practical application involved facing the violent subject, blocking a punch, delivering a return strike, and moving behind the individual while sliding an arm around his neck. Balance is broken by disengaging the knees while pushing the hips forward with a hand on the lower back. Once kneeling behind the seated subject, pressure is applied until unconsciousness is achieved within 5 – 15 seconds.

Hunter and his partner practiced the technique over and over on each other until the motions became fluid, but refrained from actually rendering partners unconscious. He remembered using the carotid restraint a few times in the field and at rock concerts upon persons experiencing violent reactions to illicit drugs, or mental patients whose psychotic behavior made them dangerous to themselves or others. On only one occasion had it not been successful. A driver under the influence of PCP was so intoxicated that the rigidity of his neck muscles prevented external pressure from blocking his arteries. Hunter and his back-up officer had to wrestle the suspect on the freeway shoulder to get him handcuffed.

The remainder of Hunter's class consisted of light sparring without pads. Now, at the rank of lieutenant he seldom engaged in hand to hand combat, but he liked the fact that during a recent training trip to Japan he observed several martial arts practitioners in their 60's, 70's, and 80's who were still training. These classes were tremendous at relieving the stress in the days following the seemingly endless writing of reports documenting the homicides, and testifying during Steinhoffer's "obstruction" trial.

Chapter 73

The training seminar had been scheduled months ago and was only one day long, but it was being held in Washington, D.C. The topic was terrorism and a special guest speaker was the world's first air marshal, a former Israeli Defense Forces officer, and debriefs of major incidents occurring in Beslin, Nece, and Paris would be featured. With the homicides having been solved the timing couldn't be better.

Hunter had planned to make it a long weekend with Ashley by sightseeing at the nation's capital, which included the Smithsonian Space Museum and George Washington's home in Mount Vernon, Virginia. She arranged some creative shift swaps and managed to work on Scott's flight to D.C., as well as their return flight home.

Thursday morning they awakened at Hunter's Newport condo and prepared for their flight. For Ashley it was all business, dressed impeccably in her blue uniform and polished black work shoes. Scott was business casual with blue collared shirt, pleated tan chinos, and black leather jacket.

"Are you bringing a firearm sweetheart?"

"Not on board, I'll check it with TSA in my luggage."

"Thanks, the check-in procedure for a non-extradition firearm in the cabin can be a hassle depending on who's the captain; and since I'm working, I had better not be late."

"No problem, we'll get there on time, and I'll be the model passenger, Ma'am."

Ashley smiled as she put the finishing strokes on her lashes with a mascara brush. Hunter loaded the trunk with their luggage and they headed off to John Wayne Airport's American Airlines terminal.

Early morning traffic was light and TSA lines were minimal. Hunter boarded the 737's main cabin and took the "D" seat on the right side of the aisle, facing the curtain separating first class. Ashley was assigned to first class, and her friend, Christie Bogner, worked Hunter's section of the main cabin. The flight was nearly full, and was scheduled for one stop at Dallas/Fort Worth, Texas.

Once the aircraft reached cruising altitude, beverage service began. Hunter browsed through a schedule for his terrorism seminar he was using as a bookmark for his Tom Clancy novel, and caught a glance of Ashley through a parting of the curtain covering first class. He gave Christie his drink order, and suddenly saw Ashley standing next to her whispering in her ear as she poured coffee for the passenger seated in seat "C." As Ashley's head was turned away from Hunter, her left hand dropped a small, folded piece of paper into his lap.

Without looking at Hunter, Ashley turned around and disappeared behind the first class curtain. Hunter discreetly opened the note inside the cover of his book. It read as follows:

"Male passenger in first class seat on right side of aisle, in row next to curtain is drunk and becoming loud. There's no air marshal on this flight. Crew is aware, I'll keep you posted."

Hunter folded the note closed and tucked it in his shirt pocket. He assumed that Ashley would be declining the passenger's beverage order, and that the fireworks in first class would be erupting shortly. There was one male flight attendant working the rear of the aircraft, but from Hunter's assessment, he was effeminate and small in stature. It was only a few minutes before 9:00 AM, and several passengers in proximity to Hunter were sleeping.

Hunter dreaded these situations. He was off duty, but not really. He possessed all the skills and training to address crisis situations, but there were always more responsibilities attached to them. The reports, court testimony, civil liability, and possibly medical treatment and rehabilitation awaited him should he elect to take any action. Added to these liabilities was the fact that an aircraft was involved, and such incidents captured media attention, both positive and negative. He would cautiously wait and hope that the guy would fall asleep.

Ashley had left the curtain slightly separated to give Hunter a limited view of the aisle and last row of seats in first class. He could hear the inebriated passenger's voice rising and some of Ashley's responses were intermittently audible in her attempt to maintain calm. Another female flight attendant working first class approached to render assistance and stood in the aisle between Ashley and the cockpit, while the passenger remained seated but animated with his hands and arms. Ashley still held the metal coffee pot she had used to fill the cup of another passenger in the last row.

The drunk rose to his feet and was now shouting his demand that Ashley prepare him a Bloody Mary. Hunter could see that he was about 6'2", weighed approximately 230 pounds, and appeared to be carrying a bowling ball stomach under the polo shirt protruding beyond his beltline. He estimated the man was 35 years old and could now see sweat droplets on his brow and upper lip.

Ashley turned in the aisle toward the cockpit door to summon the assistance of the co-pilot, and the drunk lunged with his left hand grabbing Ashley's dress at the base of her right buttocks. She reacted with a backswing of her right arm, still holding a near empty metal coffee pot, striking the right jaw of the drunkard.

Hunter had by now passed the curtain and wrapped his right arm around the man's neck. He dropped to his knees, taking him down to a seated position in the aisle, and began to apply pressure on the man's carotid arteries with his right, and now left arm that had wrapped the neck, allowing both hands to clasp to lock the hold.

Within ten seconds Hunter rendered him unconscious and rolled him onto his stomach into a handcuffing position. Anticipating problems after reading Ashley's note, Hunter had pulled an electrical plastic zip-tie from his backpack that officers used for handcuffing during mass arrests at rock concerts and demonstrations. He then threaded the zip-tie through his belt loops below his leather belt. He had seen too many newscasts of unruly passengers on airplanes being awkwardly constrained with seatbelts.

When the drunk had regained consciousness in the aisle, the pilot, Captain Charles "Chuck" Blackstone, now stood over him holding his wallet and reading his driver's license information for his report. Hunter had returned to his seat and was drinking a Diet Coke while awaiting further direction from Captain Blackstone. He wondered how many cellphone cameras had captured his face for the evening news.

~

"Mr. Giroux we will be arriving at Dallas/Fort Worth shortly where you will be handed over to federal authorities who will be waiting for you," announced Capt. Blackstone.

Hunter alerted upon hearing the man's name. He knew that he should remember it, but for the moment it escaped him. When the male flight attendant assisted the captain in lifting Giroux to his seat, the attendant used his first name "Larry," which brought Hunter's memory into focus.

Larry Giroux was now a former Orange County Sheriff's Special Deputy following his ex-girlfriend's allegations of assault related to the Jimmy Buffet concert. Through a relative's connection to a major retail chain, Giroux landed a position as a western regional director of security, and was heading to Virginia to attend introductory training in Chesapeake. Giroux was no

284

longer a serial killing suspect, but Hunter knew that his association to criminality had now been established. It would appear that Mr. Giroux's second career in security would also be jeopardized by his misuse of alcoholic beverages.

Chapter 74

Steinhoffer gazed at the setting sun through the windshield of his staff car as dusk slowly ushered in the closing of his law enforcement career. This final step in the termination process would be relinquishing of his Ford Crown Victoria to the Long Beach Police motor pool - the final perk, which he had managed to delay. He had carefully planned when minimal staffing would be present to witness this embarrassing event. He had already endured the humiliation of relinquishing his badge, I.D. card, service pistol, and uniforms. It was a complete removal of an identity normally characterized by service and honor. But to his peers he would now serve as an example of tragic consequences.

Driving northbound on the 405 freeway his mood bounced from anger to despair as he reviewed the loss he was suffering. Within a matter of weeks he had witnessed his career disintegrate, his marriage crumble, and his reputation plummet from crime fighter to criminal.

As he traveled through Irvine, he was reminded of his first chief's job for a major city, and how unceremoniously he had departed. He still believed it was the chronic battles with the city council, the police union, and the staff who never fully appreciated his talent, that were the factors ultimately contributing to the dilemma he now faced. He could not envision his life as an inmate, nor the shame of the absence of the power he had enjoyed. As Steinhoffer drew closer to Sand Canyon Road, he looked to his right toward Old Barranca Road, then down at his passenger seat where his academy pistol, a Smith & Wesson Model 19 lay, loaded with .357 magnum hollow points.

~

Midway through his graveyard shift Officer Janowitz turned his patrol car onto Old Barranca Road. His high beams reflected off the taillight lens of what appeared to be a Ford sedan. As he drew closer, he could see the sedan resembled the standard police staff car parked on the wrong side of the road under the overhanging branches of the pepper tree. Janowitz crossed the centerline of the roadway and pulled onto the shoulder of the southbound lane where he threw the toggle for his spotlights. After radioing his location and the license plate, the dispatcher sent him a follow-up unit and advised him the vehicle was registered to Long Beach PD.

Making his standard approach from the left, Janowitz' flashlight swept across the driver's side window which was covered on the inside with blood, and displayed the classic spider web shaped glass fracture of a bullet hole. Pressed against the glass appeared to be a human head, and hair matted with blood, bone fragments, and brain matter. Janowitz slowly advanced toward the windshield attempting to get a better angle for identifying the face. However, the path of the bullet had sheared off a significant portion of the left forehead, eye socket, and cheekbone, making facial identification of the victim impossible from that position. It was apparent that the occupant was deceased, giving Janowitz time to exercise care in preserving the scene.

It wasn't until his flashlight illuminated the victim's left hand that he recognized the traditional class ring with the bold letters "N A" for National Academy, signifying the bearer was a graduate of the FBI's National Academy. Janowitz remembered that his previous chief, Steinhoffer, had worn a similar ring, and that only a handful from his own department had attended. Moving his light to the victim's right hand, he found a Smith & Wesson revolver clenched with the index finger wrapped around the trigger, with the barrel resting on the bench seat. Janowitz began to feel his stomach tighten as stress mounted with his thoughts that the victim before him could be his former chief.

Following Sgt. Austin's arrival, Janowitz retrieved a small zippered pouch from the front seat and located a wallet containing a driver's license identifying Steinhoffer as the driver. In addition, he copied the serial number from the pistol, ran it through Dispatch, and confirmed that the weapon was registered to the former chief. Austin secured the scene until CSI and the coroner's office had finished, and notified the Long Beach Police administration.

Prior to leaving the scene, Austin, who held little regard for the former chief, turned to Janowitz and stated, "You know, this is the second time this guy left us a mess to clean up."

Chapter 75

The temperature reached 80 degrees on this spring day in May, and the Santa Ana winds were intermittently raising the flags to horizontal on the Civic Center's flagpoles. Hunter left the station as was his normal practice at 11:15 AM, when Ashley was in town. They would meet for lunch at that favorite spot where Japanese cuisine was "Ichiban," the first, best, or tops.

He would sit in the back with patient anticipation. She would open the door, and his heart would seem to stop. As she approached, his eyes floated downward to tawny brown bangs, flowing mane of curls, white open-neck blouse, strand of pearls, ebony skirt, and matching spiked heels. A hint of Shalimar caught up to him, and he rose to meet her eyes. The kiss, the embrace, and the moment of intimacy were greeted with smiles.

Lunch was about them. Work, finances, and issues were discarded for relationship building, and sometimes words weren't even necessary. They'd hold hands walking out to the parking lot, but today would be different. Instead of Hunter returning to work, they would make a momentary detour. They both got into his staff car. He drove down Old Barranca Road, as the radio crackled with car stops, records checks, and calls for service. They quietly watched as the tree size increased with each rotation of his tires. A tree that within a few years, would disappear with a new residential development burying its history and its horrors.

He pulled to the shoulder as dust caught the wind, and momentarily blanketed the leaves. They both got out and approached the tree. Ashley reached into her purse and pulled out two pink bows, with attached decorative cards bearing the names of Kimberly Donahue and Wendy Gilbert. Ashley tied them to separate branches, and then retrieved from her purse, a lavender colored bow and decorative card bearing the name of Lena Holmquist. She chose a different color, representing a different location, but in an act of commemorative bonding, she tied it to another branch on the pepper tree.

"How is it that so many heroic members of such a noble profession still end up hiring some breathtakingly evil people? They're like monsters with human faces." Ashley asked.

Hunter responded, "While growing up, my Dad and I would regularly watch the classic television series, Dragnet, starring Jack Webb, as Sergeant Joe Friday. Each time, he and his partner would work different assignments: robbery, homicide, bunco, etc. What stands out in my mind was the episode when they were assigned to Internal Affairs, and Friday's partner asked a similar question following the arrest of a fellow officer. Sgt. Friday's poignant answer was, "because we recruit from the human race."

Acknowledgements

There have been leaders in my thirty-four year career in law enforcement who have served as examples of strong values and sound tactics in a broad spectrum of police operations. They became my role models, demonstrating proper methods for investigating crime and managing some of the most extraordinary criminal cases. The contributions to our profession by Chief Jerry Boyd (retired), a former captain with the Irvine Police Department, and my first SWAT commander, and Deputy Chief Mike Hillmann (retired), Los Angeles Police Department have been truly outstanding, and their influence upon my own creative writing has been immeasurable.

You will also enjoy the first book in this series from
Aakenbaaken & Kent

Lincoln 9

by

Dave Freedland

When Bethany Crutchfield failed to show for Sunday brunch and her father's phone calls remained unanswered, concern was warranted. Police officers from "America's Safest City," Irvine, California, discovered a gruesome homicide scene which established Bethany as the first in a series of murders that would ultimately span over two decades. Lincoln 9 takes place in a city whose reputation for safety and affluence overshadows the fact that the relatively few homicides are among the most vicious and complex cases. Lincoln 9 follows the career of Lieutenant Scott Hunter, the consummate cop who leads a team of detectives on a mission aimed at connecting the clues and solving these crimes. The story conveys the pressures of working in an organization whose efforts result in perennial accolades for achieving the lowest numbers of violent crime. In addition, it introduces a look behind the curtain of secrecy shielding the role played by Special Weapons and Tactics (SWAT) Teams in the development of leaders.

Although all Aakenbaaken & Kent books are available online and in ebook format, we encourage you to support your local independent bookstore and buy or order from them. If you do not have an indie bookstore, you can order them from Book & Table, the independent bookstore in Valdosta, Georgia where all Aakenbaaken & Kent books are discounted 10% and shipping is free. Ordering is easy. Just email the store at:

bookandtablevaldosta@gmail.com